It's

CURTAINS

for

Tony Jones

4-30-87

All best,

Jim

CURTAINS

new and selected stories
by
James McManus

another chicago press

Published in the United States by Another Chicago
Press, Box 11223, Chicago IL 60611

Design by Linda Lake
Cover design by Michele Nosco

The pieces in this collection have appeared in the
following publications: *TriQuarterly, Another Chicago Magazine, New Directions in Prose and Poetry, Kansas Quarterly Oyez Review, Story Quarterly*. "Roque Dalton Garcia Is Dead", "The Skinner",
"The Eye of Hunan", "Torque", "North America",
"Young Seventh-World Women", "The Venturi
Effect", and "The Shack Dwellers" were first published by Syncline Press in a chapbook entitled
Antonio Salazar is Dead. "Ithaca" appears in a
somewhat different form in *Chin Music* from
Crown Publishers, Inc.

Thanks to the National Endowment for the Arts and
the Illinois Arts Council for financial assistance with
this project, and to Crown Publishers, Inc., for
permission to reprint "Ithaca".

Library of Congress Catalog preassigned Card
Number: 85-072236

ISBN: 0-9614644-0-2

Contents

Autoclysm

I didn't find out until the following morning that Reginald Dilmore was dead. Reid Wynston, at whose house we'd played poker that night, called me up. Five minutes after we'd all left the Wynstons', Dilmore's '60 Impala had slid through a red light at the Rt. 53 intersection and been caught high up and flush in the driver's side door by a Peterbilt tractor-trailer carrying a piggyback load of Four Star Farms sausage.

"Dead on arrival," Reid said. "Impala got totaled."

"You're serious, aren't you," I said. "I mean, you're not kidding."

"I'm serious as a heart attack, man," Reid said then. Then he said, "Look, gotta go. Dudes from the coroner's office are over here grilling my old man right now."

About the only thing unusual about the game out at Reid's house that night was that we hadn't been drinking—and that, I supposed, was what would get his old man off the hook. Most of our games were spent relating or concocting various successes we'd had with the local Sacred Heart girls, gambling four or five times more money than we could hope to afford, listening to the Kingsmen, and drinking until whatever Budweiser or bourbon or scotch we'd managed to purchase, or have purchased for us, ran out. But when Dilmore left the Wynstons that night he was sober.

We all were. And by one or one-thirty we were all of us ready to call it a night: we'd agreed on a cut-off, in fact, four or five hands in advance. Pat and Jack Collins and I all were up, Carl Rendecki was just about even, and Dilmore and Reid were way down. Especially Dilmore, who'd been losing all evening—getting bad cards, playing reckless with the good ones he did get, coming in second a lot. You could tell it was starting to get to him. The closest anyone could reckon was that at this point he was about sixty-five bucks in the red. Dilmore himself wasn't talking.

"It's been real," said Carl, getting up, "and it's been nice. It's just that it wasn't real nice."

"Oh, but it was," said Jack Collins. "But it was."

"Seven stud," Dilmore said, staying put. "One last hand."

"Played it four hands ago," Pat Collins said.

"Winners don't walk from the table, man," Dilmore said.

"Jesus, Dilmore," said Reid. "Don't be a dickfor."

"You know Reggie's problem?" said Carl. He held up his thumb and his index finger, pressing them tightly together, and stared right at Dilmore. "He's got this very small particle of brain lodged in his skull."

Dilmore anted up two quarters anyway and started to deal, placing four common cards face down in the middle. There was nothing we could think of to say to him.

"Three bump limit," he said, watching the quarters pile up. "Two bucks a bump."

4

He looked across the table at me. We'd never been all that fond of each other, particularly since the fourth game of the football season when he'd taken my spot in the backfield—this together with the fact that I was currently sitting on a good deal of his next three months' spending money. "Who's light?" he said.

I tossed a dollar into the pot and took out two quarters.

"What a man," Dilmore said.

"What an anos," I said.

The first card he turned was the seven of clubs. Both Collinses perfunctorily checked. So did I. Reid, yawning hugely, bet a dollar.

"Let's try a little quick kick," Dilmore said, as soon as Carl tossed in his dollar. He was smiling. "I raise it one dollar."

We threw in our money in silence.

The next card he turned was an eight, also of clubs. Reid once again bet a dollar and, once again, Dilmore raised him.

The Collinses folded, put on their coats, and walked out: you could tell they were happy to leave. Reid, always the gracious young host, nodded goodbye for the rest of us.

I'd looked at my cards while the Collinses were making their exit: a pair of red threes. I tossed in two dollars.

"Love to see it," said Dilmore, looking across at me. "Price of poker's going up fast."

"Then I guess you'll be loving to be paying to see these," I said.

"You got it," he said.

Our hard and fast rule was that there was no betting light. Reid reminded Dilmore of this. "U.I.O.G.D.," he said then. "Don't want no I.O.U.'s."

5

Dilmore said nothing. He simply flipped the next card—the four of clubs—and brought out his wallet.

"Check to the flushes," I said.

Reid once again bet a dollar.

"I see that dollar," said Carl, tossing one in, "that in all things God may be glorified."

While Dilmore was fishing around in his wallet's various compartments, I just caught a glimpse of what looked to be my old girlfriend Linda's school picture—but sideways, that quick, wasn't sure. Dilmore finally pulled out a dirty gray bill folded up to about the size of a cigarette butt. He unfolded it carefully now, laid it on top of the pot, and began taking change. The bill was a twenty.

"Kick it two dollars," he said.

It was clear there were flushes abroad, possibly straight ones, so a full boat was the least I'd be needing. And at this point I was still two long-shot cards away. Something about Dilmore's attitude, though—everything about it, in fact—made me want to stay in. So I did.

Reid also saw the two dollars, then checked. Carl dropped out.

"Take this here pot," he said, to no one in particular, "and purchase yourself a hot pork injection."

"That'd be kind of hard," Dilmore said.

"Harder the better," said Carl, counting his quarters.

Dilmore seemed dazed.

"You'd learn to love it," I said. "Turn the card."

The card was my three. The problem was that it was clubs.

Carl stood up from the table and stretched. "Let's not use the F-word now, Mr. Jimmy."

I just checked.

Reid bet a dollar, Dilmore raised two, and I

saw the three. They both looked at me. Reid raised it two more then, Dilmore raised back two, and I saw it again. By this point I figured I just about had to—all that money already just to see my last card, fifty-four bucks in the pot.

"Check to the kicker," Reid said.

Dilmore raised two again, and the three of us put in our money.

"Deal," Reid said then. "Low and slow."

"Uncleanly and bottomous," said Carl, looking on.

"Down and dirty," said Dilmore, carefully tossing our cards. I could tell he was nervous. We all were.

"Dealer takes one," he said then. As a joke.

My card, of course, was the three of spades. When we were all through betting the pot was ninety-nine dollars, easily a month's take-home pay for any of the part-time jobs we had then. Reid ended up showing a king-high club flush and Dilmore, of course, had the ace. He came in second.

Reid called me back about five minutes later. We discussed Dilmore's funeral, which was Tuesday in Naperville, and we talked for a while about how little we'd actually known him. I never did bring up the picture.

"Remember that twenty?" Reid said.

"Got it right here in my hand." I straightened it out, turned it over. Andrew Jackson looked back, upside down. You could still see rectangular creases from the way Dilmore'd had the thing folded.

"Pretend it's *my* twenty, man," Reid said then. "My old man might get nailed just for letting him drive after curfew. You know, just like don't spend it. Kind of won it on a no-brainer anyway."

"Right."

"He dealt those cards himself, man," Reid said. "Wanted to play them. It isn't, you know—no way thing like that is your fault."

"I guess so."

"Just some trucker, you know, trying to out-guess the light in that slush," Reid said then. "Don't you think? Shouldn't've even stuck around for that last hand."

"Right."

"You know, man?" Reid said.

I turned Jackson's face rightside up. "Yeah, I know."

Slip

Back to the rough ground!
Ludwig Wittgenstein

I was walking north on Michigan Avenue, headed for Jacque's. With the wind-chill factor it must have been 25° or 30° below out, but the sidewalks were crowded with bundled-up lunch-hour shoppers. At the corner of Superior Street the signal turned red and I stopped. A skinny young black kid, about thirteen or fourteen, kept walking. He was wearing green hightop sneakers and, in spite of the cold, a thin vinyl windbreaker; the bottoms of his jeans had been neatly cut into tatters. He was trying to make it across Superior ahead of the traffic, though at the same time he didn't look to be in all that much of a hurry.

As he reached the middle of the street his left foot suddenly shot up over his head, as though he were following through on a punt. His arms were thrown sideways and his right foot, too, left the ground. For a second he flailed like this in midair, frantically grabbing for some form of resistance. He came down hard on his butt, actually bounced back up two or three inches, then sat on the asphalt. By this point cars in both eastbound lanes were almost on top of him, and two women standing next to me on the curb started screaming. The drivers, however, had managed to screech to a halt.

9

The kid's back was still toward me, so I was unable to see the look on his face. Right next to him, though, running parallel to the lane divider, I could see the three-foot strip of slick, tightly packed snow that had upended him. Aside from this single patch, the asphalt was dry as a bone.

Slowly the kid picked himself up. Apparently unhurt, he grinned at the two lines of cars that had formed. Throwing his shoulders back then, his puny chest out, he placed his right forearm across his waist, his left one behind his back, and bowed deeply to the traffic, his head almost brushing against one of the bumpers.

Dozens of horns were now blaring. Out of patience, one of the drivers swerved past, shouting obscenities and gesturing at the kid through his windshield. The kid just ignored this. He faced the people standing on the other side of Superior and bowed for a second time.

Two more cars went by now, angling deliberately close to him. Still taking his time, he turned on his heel, faced my side of the street, and bowed once again. Those who were shivering there with me stared back at him, or glanced around at each other, but there was nothing we could think of to say.

Dodging a Buick, the kid finally sprinted off in the direction he'd been headed in the first place, disappearing up ahead into a cluster of pedestrians.

The light turned green for the rest of us at exactly this moment.

Picasso

She was kneeling in front of some lockers, chin up, erect, staring right past me down the third-floor north hallway. It was the first time I saw her. Her arms were raised parallel to the floor, with her white hands and fingers dangling down from her wrists. The school's maroon blazer was pulled taut across her. It loosened a little each time she breathed or lowered her arms even slightly, then stretched even tighter when she raised them back up or breathed in. I just watched her.

One of the nuns was crouching beside her, head cocked and tilted way over, checking the length of her uniform skirt. "Oh my goodness, young lady."

She made no response. Her naked knees trembled between the plaid maroon pleats and the tiles, but her very strange face didn't show it.

The nun, clucking and tsking, had her back to me, and her habit's black veil was hanging down over her shoulders. I couldn't tell which nun it was.

"Oh my my my my."

No response.

"Let me see," said the nun, standing up. "This is quite serious."

A small crowd of gawkers had started to form just behind me. I did not turn around, but I could feel them now leering and mocking her.

"There's at least four inches there," said the

nun. "Maybe five, even. Five whole inches, young lady, from that hem to the floor."

"Sister?" she said. She didn't look up. She was blushing.

"Five at least."

She continued to stare, not moving one muscle, past me, past the gawkers, at nothing.

"Remain, young lady, just as you are," said the nun, then brought out her pad of pink detention slips and started to write.

I heard some girl whisper, "It's Picasso again."

There was laughter.

"Just you stay right where you are," said the nun.

Without budging the rest of her body, she moistened her lips with her tongue.

"You'll have had that hem lowered tomorrow, I trust. Or indeed you will *not* bother coming."

She didn't look up. "I will, Sister," she said. Her words came out flat and straightforward.

The nun kept on writing. "I should very well hope so."

No response.

"Arms out and straight there, young lady. Up and straight."

She continued only to breathe, and to stare, and to blush.

Over the next six or eight weeks I went out of my way—following her in the hallways, keeping my ears open around the seniors and juniors, from time to time asking them questions—to find out just who this girl was.

At first I'd assumed that her last name was really Picasso: it was the only way her classmates would

12

ever refer to her. So that was how I referred to her too, in my mind, even later.

Her real name was Linda Krajacik. She was a junior. She'd started at St. Procopius in January, but nobody seemed to know from what school, or even what state, she had transferred. But she had Father Albin for chemistry, which meant she was one of the smart ones.

Her hair was light brown, with bangs hanging down past her eyebrows, real straight and long on the sides and in back. And real clean. It looked like she didn't use hair spray.

She didn't wear kneesocks, nylons, or penny loafers. She did not wear a senior boy's ring. She did not go to pep rallies, sock hops, basketball games, or join any language clubs. She did not get along. As far as I was able to tell, in fact, she spoke with no one at all.

Three or four times I heard her name read over the PA as one of the people who had after-school detention duty. She was one of the very few girls who made that list even once.

She lived out in Hinsdale and drove into Lisle by herself in a red MG Midget.

She never ate lunch. She was tall. She wore moccasins.

Her father was supposedly no longer living with her and her mother—either that or he'd died. Her mother worked for CBS News.

She had once come to school wearing a braided and black leather headband.

I was standing at one of the urinals in the second-floor john. On a tile to my left, neatly printed in green magic marker, were the words:

HONORABLE GOOK SAY PICASSO
SUCK THE BIG HIPPIE DICK

I desperately wanted to get it rubbed off, or at least cross part of it out with my pen, but the john was too crowded. I zipped up my pants and walked out.

By the time I went back the next morning, the janitors had done the job for me. (At St. Procopius, only the most harmless graffiti would last more than a day or two.) The glossy finish of the entire white tile had been sanded, and no trace of green ink was left.

I figured her face was the reason they called her Picasso.

Her eyes were dark gray, with maybe some green added in. I never had got a close look.

One eye looked wider sometimes, and a bit higher up, than the other, and from certain angles they seemed to be too far apart.

Her nose wasn't centered exactly, either, and her cheekbones looked tilted.

As in a Picasso, I guessed.

I was hitchhiking on Ogden Avenue on my way home from Synder's, the pool hall in Naperville. It was the last week of March, Friday night, around twelve-fifteen or twelve-thirty. There were not many cars on the road, and the ones that were out weren't stopping.

Mattingly Oldsmobile's lights had just switched themselves off when a little red sports car finally pulled over. Picasso.

"Get in," she said, holding the passenger's door halfway open. "Hurry up now."

"The Last Time" was playing on a small black and chrome tape deck. I never had seen one before.

"Thanks for stopping," I said.

She shifted into first and roared off. "It's cold out," she said.

"There's cops along here," I said, then immediately wondered how I could possibly know that.

She was already doing around fifty-five, sixty. "Is there?" she said.

I nodded, then shrugged. "Sometimes, I guess."

"You go to St. Procopius, don't you?"

I was surprised, but just nodded.

She stared straight ahead at the road, dimming her brights for an oncoming car, shifting twice.

"So you're Laughlin Madden," she said.

I looked over at her. "How'd you know that?"

"Know what?"

We had to talk loud, almost shout, because of the music.

"I'm Jim," I said then. "Laughlin James."

"Right."

She was wearing a fringed buckskin jacket, what looked to be an inside out sweatshirt, and bell bottoms. I was doing my best not to stare at her.

"The Last Time" ended while we were stopped at a light, and "Good Times" came on. When the light changed to green, I watched while she shifted and clutched through the gears.

"You're a sophomore," she said.

I admitted it.

"So you're what? Just sixteen?"

"Not till July." I was dying.

She put her right hand on my shoulder, held it a couple of seconds, then put it back down on the shifter. I could feel myself starting to sweat.

"You're young for your age, then," she said.

We had stopped at another red light. I wanted to tell her that my birthday was July 26, and that this was also Mick Jagger's birthday. I didn't.

"I guess so," I said. "For a sophomore . . ."

She stared at me, smiling. I looked back for a second, meeting her eyes, then blinked and stared out through the windshield. The light facing Warrenville Road still was green.

She produced a thin, twisted, wrinkled-up cigarette now from inside her jacket and held it up proudly between us. "Do a reefer with me, Laughlin James?"

Our light had turned green, and she shifted into first and took off.

"Sure," I said, my head snapping back. "A reefer would really be great."

Still holding onto the reefer, she shifted from first into second. "Good," she said. "Good."

"I could use one," I said.

She placed the reefer between her thick lips, took a small blue box of matches off the dashboard, then shifted from second to third. "Shift for me, will you?" she said.

We were, I knew, now in third—I'd been watching her carefully—so fourth would be simply straight back. I'd never operated a manual transmission before—though I *could* drive my dad's automatic—but could see what the gear pattern was on the shifter.

"Ready?" she said.

"Yeah." I was desperate to appear nonchalant. "Go ahead."

She pushed in the clutch and I jerked the stick back. For the first couple of inches it came pretty smoothly, but it caught near the middle and groaned.

The struck match now lit up her face. "Pull," she said, lighting the reefer.

I got the stick free by shaking and pushing it sideways, then finally got it to come all the way back.

The engine roared loud as she let out the clutch and we quickly lost all our momentum. I had hit second.

"Missed it," she said, holding her breath.

She shook out the match, shook her head.

"I thought——"

Our fingers touched twice as she passed me the reefer.

"Me too," she said.

She pushed in the clutch one again, eased the stick toward my thigh, then shoved it back hard into third. "Smoke it," she said.

Between my two fingers, the reefer seemed flimsy and weightless. For some reason I'd imagined them to be more like regular cigarettes. The lit end flared up and popped when I dragged, which surprised me, and I had to work hard not to cough.

"The Under Assistant West Coast Promotion Man" came on as I carefully passed back the reefer.

Picasso took two little drags, inhaled, took another one, then wanted to know, "Where you headed?"

"Home," I said, exhaling. My left eye was watery. "Lisle."

I looked out the window, at the glass of the window itself, then back at Picasso. She was trying to pass me the reefer.

I took it. I concentrated this time on taking my drag without coughing.

"You're home, then," she said.

I looked out and saw we were now in the west end of Lisle, out by Dooleys. Oakview, the subdivision I

17

lived in, was eight blocks south of the next light, at Main Street.

"Want to go for a drive?" said Picasso. She exhaled a long plume of smoke.

I desperately needed to cough, but I didn't. "I guess so," I said. As she had ben doing, I answered while holding my breath.

"That mean yes?"

"Sure," I said. "Great."

"Where to?" she said.

I exhaled and passed her the reefer. "You mean, to where?"

"Riiight."

"Well, nowhere really . . ."

There was a silence now. Picasso looked over at me and blew her bangs out of her eyes. I tried to look back, but looked down.

"Doesn't matter?" she said.

I nodded, then said, "I mean, no."

"Any ideas, though?"

"Where to, you mean?"

She shook her head, *whew*ed, took a drag. "That's right, man," she said.

"Up to you," I said then. "You decide."

At Ogden and Main she turned left, and we headed on out toward the tollway.

"Your name's Linda," I said. "I mean, right?" I hardly could call her Picasso.

"K."

"That's How Strong My Love Is" came on. I just nodded.

"For Krajacik," she said.

"Oh."

She touched a small lever on the side of the tape deck and made "Satisfaction" come on.

18

"Who calls you K.?" I said then.

We were now on the eastbound entrance ramp to the tollway, and she shifted into third and accelerated. "You do," she said. Then she turned up the volume still further. "Made loud to be played loud," she said.

I said nothing.

Picasso quickly brought the Midget's speedometer to just under ninety, and I could feel the vibrations and whines of this speed on my skin. I think—though I can't be that sure—I was scared. We listened to "Satisfaction" two times, watched the tollway flash past through the conical beams of the headlights, didn't say much. Only our knuckles would touch as we passed one another the reefer.

When we got near the toll booths at Oak Brook, Picasso rolled down her window and flicked what was left of the reefer outside.

"We're cool now," she said.

I said, "Great."

The huge banks of lights made me squint as we entered the plaza. Picasso pulled down her visor and headed for the exact-change lanes on the left.

"Think they've got enough lights on?" she said.

"Really," I said.

As she arched up her torso to dig her hands into her pockets I could make out her breasts and her nipples pushing up through the white sweatshirt. I quickly looked down at the shifter.

After paying the toll she drove about two hundred yards past the plaza, made a fast, squealing U-turn between a pair of yellow and red rubber cones, then headed back toward the westbound exact-change booths.

"Got a nickel?" she said.

I pulled all my change from my pockets. I'd won almost four dollars that night playing quarter-half nineball, so there was a lot of it. I felt pretty proud of myself.

Picasso opened her hand next to mine. "Merci," she said.

I picked out a nickel and stared at it, trying to think what to say. I said, "Here."

She took the nickel, jangled it together with the coins she already had in her hand, and tossed them all into the hopper, then began to accelerate as soon as the gate had swung open.

"I owe you a nickel," she said.

There was nothing I could think of to say to her.

A half-minute later she touched my left thigh with her pinkie and pointed to a small shelf under the dashboard that served, I guessed, as a glove compartment. "Cigarettes," she said. "Gotta have one."

I reached around in the darkened compartment and brought out a hardpack of Marlboros.

"Want one?" she said.

"For a nickel . . ."

"Sold," she said. And somehow I also said, "Sold."

"I think we've got it backwards," she said. "Or something. But give me one anyway, quick. And you take one."

I pulled two Marlboros from the half-empty pack, lit them both without faltering, and handed one over.

"Muchas gracias," she said. "You're a dear."

I wanted to ask her now whether she'd had Mr. Dennerlein last year for geometry, but I remembered that it was only her first semester at St. Procopius. I wanted to ask where her father was. I wanted to tell her that if she didn't want me to call her Picasso, or even think of her as Picasso, I wouldn't.

"The Under Assistant West Coast Promotion Man" came on again, and we sat there and smoked without talking.

"How come I dig you so much, Laughlin James?" she said finally. She sounded as if she was serious.

I couldn't answer.

"Really," she said, touching my hand for a second. "What do you think?"

"Do you?" I said. "I don't know."

"'Cause we're stoned?"

"Maybe," I said.

"Just kidding, you know."

Another long silence.

"I just can't figure it out, though," she said. "Really can't."

"How come 'Laughlin James'?" I said then.

Picasso just smiled.

"I like you too," I said. "I mean, you know . . ."

We were now on the Lisle exit ramp.

"I just can't figure it out," said Picasso.

She turned onto Main Street, passed Route 53, and headed through town out toward Oakview.

"Saint Procopius, man," she said then. She had hit all six syllables hard.

We both crushed our Marlboros out in the ashtray.

"Really," I said.

Picasso yawned hugely and put her small hand on my forearm. I realized I had an erection. She rubbed her cool palm back and forth a few times, patted my thigh, then put her hand back on the wheel.

"Better tell me how to get you back home now," she said.

* * *

21

Home, in bed, when I tried to recall what she'd looked like, I was unable to get her face to stand still. It would either start shimmering in and out of focus or turn away from me altogether.

I wondered how she'd known what my name was.

I could still see her dropping me off: squeezing my shoulder two times, turning the volume way down on the tape deck, looking past me up at my house, saying "See you."

I was pleased that I'd finally smoked grass.

The way that her white, veined, small hand had looked gripping the shifter kept reappearing, and riffs from "The Last Time" played over and over. I was unable to stop it.

Nor was I able to picture very successfully what her breasts would look like.

Monday, during my nine-o'clock study hall, after making real sure that no one I knew was around, I went into the art books corner of the library and looked up Picasso.

There was only one book, and it consisted entirely of small reproductions. About one out of ten was in color.

I never had seen a Picasso before. The paintings, to me, seemed like the work of more than one artist. They were not what I'd've called beautiful.

Some of the faces, however, did remind me somewhat of Picasso's—I could see how the juniors had come up with the name. ("Straight off some fucking Picasso, man," one guy had said.)

In the *Portrait of Maya with a Doll*, for example, the little girl's features were literally all over the place. It was almost as if you were seeing the front of her face and the side simultaneously.

The *Portrait of Kahnweiler* was printed in color, and I laughed when I saw it. Even here I could see the similarities, the nature of the exaggeration. I got the point.

I also noticed that Picasso didn't put all that much in his pictures besides the women and men he was painting. It was like nothing else mattered or something.

I looked at *Guernica*, which took up two pages. I remember wondering what it looked like in color.

Les Demoiselles d'Avignon made me nervous.

I put the book back on the shelf and left before somebody noticed me.

I didn't see her again until Wednesday, although I'd been on the lookout for her all week. She was in the long narrow hallway outside the physics lab.

"Laughlin James," she said, taking my arm.

She was, as always, alone, but a whole class of juniors was filing by out of the lab. I didn't know how to address her.

"How are you?" I said.

"Not too bad," she said. "What about you, Laughlin James?"

"Okay," I said. "Good."

She took my shoulder then and moved me out of the flow in the hallway. "We're moving," she said. "Up to Winnetka or somewhere. I'm starting at New Trier on Monday."

"What?"

"What do you say you and me go for a drive then?" she said. "To celebrate sort of. You know, for old times' sake."

"You and your mother?" I said.

"Me and my mother."

"What do you mean *moving*, though? I mean, you just moved here."

Here, to me, in the light of the hallway, her face looked incredibly beautiful.

"Moving," she said.

I looked around at the class of smart juniors still filing out of the lab, at Picasso, at the stacks of locked cabinets where the chemicals and instruments were stored.

"When?"

"I just told you," she said. "Saturday morning."

"Oh." I felt woozy.

"My old lady got transferred again."

"And you're moving *already*?"

"Laughlin James, this happened weeks ago."

"Then why, if——"

"Got transferred the first week of March."

"Oh," I said then. "Didn't know."

"Of course not," she said. "No one did." Her gestures and tone were implying that all this should make perfect sense.

"What about finals?" I said.

"All been worked out."

"Albin's too?"

"Everything's all been worked out."

I said nothing. It was the first time we'd stood face to face, and I could tell that, even in moccasins, she was only about a half an inch shorter than me—at the most.

"Anyway," she said. "Want to go for that drive?"

"Sure," I said. "Now?"

"Of course not *now*," she said, wincing. "Thursday night. Tomorrow's my last day of school."

I stood up as straight as I could, but said nothing.

"Or maybe today should be," she said, sort of half to herself. "Now that I think of it . . ."

"Fine," I said then. My eyes were lined up with her eyebrows.

"That mean yes?"

"I guess so," I said. "Thursday night?"

"Jeez, Laughlin James. Yes or no?"

"What time, I mean."

"You ask me what time now"—she put both her hands on my shoulders—"by saying what night?"

"What?"

She took her hands off of my shoulders. "'Bout seven?"

"Good," I said. "Yeah, seven's good."

"Good, then. I'll see you at seven."

"Okay."

"And I'm glad you said yes."

"You remember how to get to my house?"

"Yes I do, sir."

"Seven, then?"

"Seven. Are *you* glad?"

"That I said yes?" I said.

She now moved her face even closer, and I could see that her skin was translucent.

"I'll see you," she said.

I shaved Thursday night after dinner with my new Techmatic cartridge. I can remember thinking about the White Sox's chances that season: they had lost again that afternoon. I was nervous.

I washed my hair in the shower, soaped my whole body, shaved my neck and my chin one more time.

I combed my hair forward and down while it

dried, and I brushed my teeth twice. I also used extra deoderant.

In my room I sat on the bed and read the back of the *Out of Our Heads* album cover: *It's a new ROLL-ING STONES album, strictly OUT OF their heads, and out of those extremely five talented heads come twelve great new sides recorded in LONDON, CHICAGO and HOLLYWOOD.* . . .

I put on my blue jeans and zipped up my black high-heeled mod boots, then pulled the jeans' cuffs down and over.

If Picasso asked me where I wanted to drive to, I planned to say Old Town—either there or the Route 16 drive-in.

I snuck into my parents' room and borrowed a pack of my father's Old Golds.

I stood in front of my mirror and examined my stomach and chest muscles, turning and flexing them, watching as the shape of each sinew was defined by the light. Then I flexed both my forearms and biceps.

My face, I thought, looked all right, but my hair wasn't long enough yet.

I put on my orange and blue paisley shirt.

When Picasso picked me up, at ten after eight, she was wearing brown leather driving gloves, the buckskin jacket she'd had on Friday night, and a navy blue mini-skirt. "I Heard It Through the Grapevine" was on the radio.

"I'm late," she said. "Sorry."

I'd told my parents I had to work that night with three of my classmates on a joint presentation of a history project: we had twenty-five pages to get written and typed by the morning, so there was a good chance I'd be out pretty late. Since a quarter to seven I'd been waiting downstairs with my two navy blue spiral notebooks, looking down the block for the Midget. I'd called Picasso's house twice, but no one had answered.

"No problem," I said.

We drove out of Oakview and headed toward Ogden. She did not ask me where we should go.

"Had to drop my old lady off in the Loop," she said then. "It's my birthday, you know."

"I didn't," I said. "Happy birthday."

"Well?"

I kissed her right cheek. She turned her head then, keeping her eyes on the road, and we kissed—she kissed me—on the lips.

"Happy birthday," I said.

"Merci, monsieur."

"If I'd known I'd've gotten you something."

"I'm sure that you would have."

I was doing my best not to stare at her legs, or even to glance at them. She was not wearing nylons. "I would have," I said.

"Knock On Wood" came on now, and Picasso turned right onto Ogden. "You think I'm jukin' you, don't you, Laughlin James?"

"What makes you say that?"

When she was through shifting gears, she felt around under her seat and brought up her wallet. She opened it, turned it rightside up, and presented it to me. "War baby," she said.

Her driver's license appeared through a clear plastic window: there was just enough light left to read it.

"That's today, sir," she said.

Her birth date was 04-06-50.

"You're . . . seventeen, then," I said. For some reason I'd assumed she'd be sixteen. "According to this . . ."

She took back the wallet. "That is correct, sir," she said.

Again I wanted to tell her that my own birthday was July 26.

"Private party at my house," she said. "Wanna come?"

"Sure."

"Or am I too old and scraggly now to be worth it. ?"

I took out my pack of Old Golds and offered her one. I just couldn't answer her question.

"No thanks," she said.

I lit an Old Gold for myself, took a drag. We drove east on Ogden in silence. What I wanted to ask her was how she had known who I was Friday night, how she'd found out my first name was Laughlin—a secret I guarded so closely. I wanted to tell her that I didn't mind if she called me that, but that Jim might be better. I also couldn't help wondering if we were going to have some sort of sex.

"In between suburbs again," she said. The sign we were passing said WELCOME TO WESTMONT, POP. 3100.

"That's me all over," she said.

I turned then and stared at the back of the sign.

"Don't you think, Laughlin James?"

"You mean, with all this moving you're doing?" I said.

"That's what I mean," said Picasso.

As we drove by the Westmont Tasty Freeze stand, an aqua '60 Impala pulled along side of us. There were five or six guys in the car.

"Hey fuckface," one shouted. They'd rolled down their windows.

My own window was three-quarters closed, and I resisted the temptation to roll it now all the way up.

"That's you, turd, that I'm talkin' to."

I pretended that nothing was happening.

"She eats me, man."

I had no idea what to do. Since the Midget was in the left lane, they were right up on top of my window.

"You blow me too, motherfuck."

I was scared. I stared as hard as I could at a spot about six inches under their door handle, trying to think what to say.

"You hear me?"

The Impala now swerved even closer. I was sure they were going to sideswipe us.

"Here you go, asshole. Eat some of this shit."

Part of a hotdog bounced off my window, smeared ketchup there, fell behind us.

"You useless little faggot gizz guzzler."

At this point Picasso reached over and showed them her raised middle finger. I couldn't believe it.

From the Impala there were crazed whoops and shrieks.

"That's right, bitch! I could *use* some strange pussy tonight!"

All of a sudden Picasso downshifted and hit the brakes hard. I looked up and saw a Du Page County Sheriff's patrol car stopped just ahead of us. Its left-hand turn signal was flashing.

Picasso just stared straight ahead, staying the appropriate distance in back of the squad car, and followed it onto a side street. The Impala continued up Ogden.

Picasso now turned off the radio. We followed

the squad car in silence for five or six blocks. Picasso turned right then and headed back over toward Hinsdale.

"Amazing assholerics," she said.

I just nodded.

"Just incredible."

I tore a page out of one of my notebooks, rolled down my window halfway, and wiped off the short streak of ketchup.

"Danke," she said.

"Nous y voici," said Picasso, leading me into her living-room. She was wearing dark blue high heels, but with my mod boots on I still seemed at least slightly taller.

"Okay," I said. "Right."

She took off the buckskin jacket and tossed it over the back of a chair. "I'll be in in a second," she said.

I looked at my hands, God knows why, then listened while her heels clicked away down the hall.

There were four or five chairs in the room, an enormous green corduroy couch, two blonde wooden lamp tables, a beige and blue carpet, a color TV set, a fireplace, a mahogany stereo console, a globe.

I sat down on one of the arms of the couch but stood back up right away.

That week's *Life* was on one of the lamp tables. The cover showed a sidewalk in downtown Hanoi with people standing chest-deep in a row of tiny little bomb shelters next to what looked to be manhole covers. It looked really strange. And the name on the subscription label was E. K. Hadley. Why not Krajacik? I wondered. And then all of a sudden it struck me that every piece of furniture in the room seemed to be exactly in place: Picasso was supposed to be moving. It convinced me that something was up.

Picasso came into the room. She had a glass in each hand and was balancing a huge blue ceramic ashtray on her forearms. She was barefoot.

"Rum and coke," she said, handing me one of the glasses. "It's all we've got left."

I tried to find some flaw in her skin, some red spot or pimple. No luck.

"Thank you," I said.

She put the ashtray down on the couch. I looked at her legs. They looked strong.

"Cheers," she said, turning and facing me.

We clinked our glasses together.

"Cheers," I said.

She sat down next to the ashtray and took a long sip of her drink. I tasted mine. The rum cut through the taste of the Coke and surprised me.

"Sit," she said then, getting up.

I sat on the couch, watching her crossing the room and lifting the top of the console. The short knitted dress rose up and clung to her butt.

"When are you actually moving?" I said.

She did not turn around. "Actually," she said. She slid an album out of its jacket, blew on it, lowered it onto the turntable. Dust crackled through two big speakers, then Marianne Faithfull's version of "As Tears Go By" started playing.

"We already moved," said Picasso.

"So but, what about all of your furniture?"

She returned to the couch and sat down. "Rented," she said.

We both took long sips of our drinks.

"Good stuff," I said.

"Comes with the house," said Picasso. "The furniture, I mean. Not the booze."

I said nothing. Her long calves and thighs continued to confront me, and I continued to try to ignore them.

"My old lady's working for NBC News," she said then.

I wanted to ask what her mother's new job was, or whether she still had the same one. I wanted to ask if she'd figured out yet why she liked me. I wanted to ask where her dad was.

"Still?" I said. "I mean, is she——"

"Yeah," she said. "Still."

I lit two Old Golds now and handed her one. She said nothing.

I tasted my drink again. It was starting to get to me now. I guessed I was too used to beer.

"When are *you* moving?" I said.

"Saturday morning," she said. "I wish we had some *real* smoke tonight."

"Really," I said.

"But we don't."

She snuffed out her cigarette then, moved the ashtray onto the floor, and slid over, pressing her thigh right against me.

"Kiss," she said then. That was all.

She opened her mouth when I kissed her, turned her head sideways, and pushed her wet tongue against mine. She tasted like vaguely sweet cigarettes. I kissed her as hard as I could.

She stopped and sat up then, resting her drink on the lamp table. I leaned down and put out my cigarette.

When we kissed again this time, Picasso put one of her hands on the side of my head: the other one held my right biceps. I kept my eyes closed. The wool dress moved over her under my hands.

She pulled out her tongue and sat up. My erection was caught against the back of my zipper, and I needed to move it. I reached for my drink.

"Happy birthday," I said.

"Sip, s'il vous plait."

I gave her my glass. She took two little sips, then stood up.

"I like you very much, Laughlin James."

I looked at her legs, at her knees, trying to think what to say.

She handed my glass back and began to unbutton her dress. I remember concluding that she was doing what she was doing because I hadn't asked *why*.

"Help me," she said.

I put down my glass, picked it back up, took one last sip, then another, then finally stood up and faced her.

She began right away to unbutton my shirt, keeping her forearms far enough apart for me to reach past them. My knees and my elbows felt wobbly. My knuckles and palms grazed her chest.

Her first two buttons came open without too much problem. I still had two, three, or four more to go, though, before reaching the waist of her dress, then two or three more after that. My fingers felt stiff as five cues.

She pulled back from me now, quickly moved past me and switched off the lamp, then moved back to where she'd been standing. I hadn't budged. Then she drew both her arms from the top of the dress and pulled it off over her head.

I stood still and watched while she unhooked her bra. I was hoping she'd smile, or something like that, but she didn't. I took off my shirt.

All she had on now were dark-colored panties. In the light from the hallway her breasts looked much more 3-D, and at the same time more delicate, than I'd expected real breasts would look——though it's hard to say *what* I expected.

"You," I said. Her nipples were small dark-gray thimbles. "I . . ."

She took my shirt and tossed it on top of her dress on the floor.

I stared at her thighs and her navel. I also could vividly picture the first time I saw her. My erection was painful.

"I?" said Picasso.

Her fingers were soft, moist, and cold, and I breathed out real hard when she touched me.

"You have a good body," she said.

Barely touching each other, and still standing up, we started to kiss one more time. Picasso's strange eyes stayed wide open.

I heard a car screech to a halt down the block, and I waited for the sound of the impact. There was none. I wondered whether the guys in the Impala could have spotted her car in the driveway.

She turned us around then and began lowering us onto the couch, tilting us sideways and backward, easing me down by the shoulders, keeping her tongue in my mouth, maneuvering us in such a way that when we finally stopped turning and sinking she was stretched out full-length in front of me, her head on my left, and I was kneeling down on the floor.

We continued to kiss. My left hand was now on her forehead, my right thumb just brushing the lower left edge of her panties. And Picasso was moving around. It was strange. The skin on the rise of her thigh felt as cool and as smooth as formica.

It finally dawned on me now that I was about to have sexual intercourse.

I knew that the most important thing was to stay nonchalant, to act like I'd been through all this stuff many times. The biggest problem I could foresee at this point was that my pants were still on, and there seemed to be no way to get free from her long enough to get out of them.

Picasso was acting like this wasn't much of a problem. She'd unfastened our tongues and our mouths and was guiding my face toward her chest. In the meantime she'd also raised her left leg against the back of the couch, causing my hand to slip down. When she let her leg fall again and raised up her hips, the cool silk crotch of her panties was forced up against my wet palm.

I arched up my palm on my fingertips. Her pussy, just underneath, was literally hot. I couldn't believe it.

"Laughlin James," said Picasso.

I massaged her crotch with the ball of my palm, using the motion I'd've used if she'd just been struck there by a fastball. At the same time I moved my lips and my tongue back and forth between her nipples, brushing them in a series of miniature triangles, concentrating hard on giving them equal amounts of attention. It amazed me how difficult it was to coordinate the two operations.

I felt my head being coaxed toward her stomach. My nose was way down by her navel before I figured out what she was up to.

I decided that my best course of action would be to keep moving down on my own, using the miniature triangles as I went, but to stop only when I'd reached her right knee. This would give me some time to get my bearings, plan my next measures—maybe even unbuckle my belt—before having to turn and head back up her thigh.

The aroma surprised me as I made my way down past her pussy. I'd been aware for two or three minutes that something had smelled funny, but it shocked me that this was the source. It smelled like a cross between shrimp, warm sweat, and a freshly mown lawn.

Picasso now arched up her back, slipped both thumbs inside her panties, and slid them right down off her hips. The smell now got stronger, and I couldn't help wondering whether all this was normal.

Without hesitation—any more waiting, I knew, would give away what I was thinking—I pulled the panties the rest of the way off her legs and tossed them back onto the carpet.

I had to admit that her pussy looked interesting, especially the way her navel was centered so neatly above it. There were so many contours and rises! Her ribcage was showing, and beyond this her breasts, now so much smaller, had spread out across her, blocking my view of her shoulders. Her chin, pointing up, was at the midpoint between them.

Her right foot dropped down to the floor while I took in the view, and I could feel her small toe pressing against my right knee. I figured this was a signal: let's go.

I'd been able to gather by then—from magazines, paperbacks, offhand observations in Snyder's, the backs of some poker decks—that a woman's most sensitive spot was her clitoris. They were "just like small cocks," some guy had said. From dictionaries I'd also gotten a general idea of the whereabouts and functions of ovaries, vulvas, aureolas, cervixes, vaginas, montes, and labia.

Picasso moaned and breathed in as soon as my tongue touched her labia. They were already wet, it turned out. The smell was there too, but from this range it seemed a lot sweeter. She tasted like sugary liver.

"Mr. Madden," she said.

Keeping my hands on her thighs, I started to search for her clitoris. Her hands were again on my head, and she was using them now to control just how hard I pressed down, where my mouth would go next, and how long I stayed at each spot. It was strange.

After two or three minutes of thoroughly searching her, though, I started to wonder if Picasso in fact *had* a clitoris. Because so far, even with her hands as my guide, I'd found nothing. The way she was moaning and writhing around, however, and from the tone of her voice when she called out my name, you'd've thought that I'd already found it.

Confused, somewhat pissed, I searched harder.

And but all of a sudden I felt my jawbone and neck being squeezed by her thighs. All I could move was my tongue.

"Laughlin James," she said then, almost calmly. She was shaking.

And then, just as suddenly, she had opened her legs and was pulling me up toward her head.

When I tried to stand up this gargantuan cramp in my thigh jerked me sideways. It disappeared, however, as soon as I straightened my leg. I was lucky.

I unbuttoned my jeans and Picasso reached up and unzipped them. Her breathing seemed louder now, and I realized the record was over. I could hear my own breathing too. It was weird.

I pushed down my jeans and my shorts and felt her cool hand on my cock. I hoped she would think it was big enough. She turned her hand over and brushed it along the bottom with the backs of her fingers. Then she grabbed it again and hung on.

I fought not to come.

"Hurry," she said, letting go.

I knelt on the couch just below her. The insides of her knees were touching the outsides of mine. I was shaking.

"I'm on the pill," she said then.

I knew what she meant, what her point was, but I couldn't respond. All I wanted to know was whose responsibility it was to get my erection inside her.

"Don't worry," she said.

I just nodded.

"Everything's cool."

I decided that to wait any longer would betray my virginity. I leaned down and forward until my chest touched her breasts. Then, raising my hips up, I aimed my cock at the spot where I figured the opening was. Then I pushed down as hard as I could.

My cock glanced off bone and bent sideways. It stayed bent that way for about a third of a second, then finally snapped straight. The pain ground my molars together.

Picasso said nothing. She was doing her best, I could tell, not to laugh.

I raised myself up, getting set, and then tried it more gently this time.

Didn't work.

"Jeez," said Picasso.

I knew that she knew now.

Picasso bit down on my shoulder—first gently, then harder—when I tried to get up. I assumed that, in her disgust, she wanted me off of her, off the couch, back in Lisle, and out of her life altogether. She actually bit me for eight or ten seconds before she let go. Then she growled. Her right hand slid down between us and grabbed what was left of my hardon. She was licking the spot where she'd bit me.

"Move back," she said then, using her left arm to guide me back down her. "Okay."

She tilted her hips up and pulled me back toward her, guiding my cock with her right hand, sort of hoisting me up with the other. It hurt.

The problem, I thought, was that my cock was still pointed forward, toward her head, and not down, and that as long as she held it this way she never would get it inside her. It would be like trying to shove a pool cue straight down into one of the pockets while the cue was still flat on the table.

The next thing I knew I was in her and something slippery and warm and bizarre was clenching and releasing itself along the sides of my cock. I was shocked.

I am doing it, I thought. I have done it!

I felt her heels digging into the base of my spine, heard her husky exhaling, before I remembered I was supposed to be screwing her.

"Ummm," she said. "God."

I shoved myself forward and down and immediately felt myself coming.

"Shit," I said, whispering. "Jesus."

She rose up to meet me, poised there against me a second, then slid back down off me again. Her heels dug in deeper. Again.

I shivered, felt awful, and came.

Her pussy made a suck-slurping noise as I tried to pull out, but her legs wouldn't let me. I tried to think of something to say to convince her that, with me, things like this usually went . . . differently. But I couldn't.

The phone rang now, so up-close and loud that I jumped.

Picasso turned over a little, reached back over her head, and answered it before the second ring started. She seemed not to mind what had happened.

"Hello."

I lay still within her.

"Hi," she said. "Fine."

I could hear the other voice vibrating through the receiver, but I couldn't make out whether it was a man's or a woman's.

"Okay."

There were ten- or twelve-second pauses before she would answer again. She had lowered her legs and was rubbing my spine with her knuckles. I tried to relax. It occurred to me once or twice that I'd pleased her, but I knew right away that I hadn't.

"I'll try to remember that, Daddy," she said.

That surprised me.

"Those were *her* suitcases, though. Are you nuts?"

I lifted my head. We looked at each other. No signal.

"Yeah," she said then. "I mean *no*. No of course not."

She put her index finger over my lips. There was no way to tell what she thought.

"I guess so," she said.

The pauses were longer now before she would answer.

"Always am."

Then: "Always do."

I could feel the weird tugging sensation again on my cock. I had to piss badly. I tried to imagine what her father looked like. Or her mother. I could feel her heart beating.

"You're kidding."

She started to move underneath me, rocking me gently and slowly, tilting her crotch up and down. I could smell her warm sweat and perfume.

"Ten o'clock."

I could also smell her pussy again.

"I've gotta go too," she said finally. "Got a million things still left to pack."

My cock had started to ache on the inside and continued to sting on the outside. I could feel it begin to get harder. I did not have to piss any more.

"Fine," she said. "Fine."

Then: "Don't *worry*. It's all written down on that pad."

Her father went on now for over a minute.

"And I know that," she said. "And I will."

She kissed the receiver. "You too," she said. "Bye."

She hung up. "Exactly where were we?" she said.

I eased myself further up into her. "That your father?"

"Oh yeah," she said, pushing back. "Sure, I remember."

I pulled back and shoved and pulled back, trying to build up some rhythm. I could sense that this time my cock would stay hard a lot longer.

"Laughlin James Madden," she said. She had her eyes closed but was smiling.

The harder I screwed her, however, the farther her hips inched away from me, and the tangle of pants at my knees made it impossible to inch up the couch to stay with her while at the same time maintaining my rhythm.

"Move back," she said, kissing my shoulder.

We shimmied ourselves down the couch till my toes touched the arm. I dug in.

"All set?"

"I think," I said. "Yeah."

She raised her hands over her head, braced them against that arm, and we both started pushing off hard.

More than anything now I wanted my buddies at Snyder's and Proco to know what was happening. Not tonight, of course, but eventually. Not for me to have to announce it, or for Picasso to tell anyone, but for the guys to somehow find it all out on their own. And then for me to *still* never mention it.

"That's *it*," said Picasso, taking short fast hard breaths through her mouth. "Laughlin *James*."

She brought her arms down and kneaded the sides of my hips, then called out my name one more time. I said nothing.

Later I raised myself up on my hands and looked at her face, at her body. She appeared to be concentrating now on receiving me into herself as gingerly as she could. Her trembling, though, and the droplets of sweat on her chest only seemed to encourage me, to add to my energy, and we continued like this for some time. I couldn't believe what was happening.

In the dark and the light from the hallway, the way she was twisting and wincing, her damp hair pushed back off her forehead, her strange face turned upward and sideways, she actually looked like a Picasso.

We took the tollway back from her house to Lisle.

Picasso had brushed her hair, put on a gray V-neck sweater and a pair of black corduroy jeans and her moccasins, and made two peanut-butter-and-honey sandwiches to take with us. We were drinking skim milk out of a large Hellman's jar.

"Also rented," she said, holding the jar up.

42

As we came to the toll booth I counted out a quarter, four dimes, and a nickel—all my change. I gave her a dime and a quarter and stacked the other four coins on the dashboard.

"Thanks," she said, picking them up. She slid them down into her pocket. The dime and the quarter she held with her lips.

There was a clock over one of the phone booths, and I remember how much it surprised me that it was only five minutes after eleven.

Picasso tossed the dime and the quarter into the hopper, waited for the light to turn green, and roared off.

"It's early," I said.

She switched on the radio then, and we just caught the last part of "Watchtower."

"Damn," said Picasso.

"A friend of mine just bought a Stratocaster," I said.

"Did he?" she said. But she really didn't sound all that interested.

The news came on now—something to do with some Buddhists setting themselves on fire—and Picasso began switching stations. After three or four tries she found "Rain."

"What do you want to do tomorrow?" I said. It was the first time I'd brought up the subject. The only things we'd discussed since we got off the couch were cigarettes, how hungry we were, where the bathroom was located, how much she still had left to pack.

Picasso looked over at me and took a small bite of her sandwich. She started to answer, then put her index finger in front of the lips to show she was chewing.

In the lights from a car we'd just passed I could just make out a trace of the ketchup smear on my window.

"Never talk with your mouth full," said Picasso, still chewing and swallowing. "Right?"

I passed her the jar and she drank.

"Maybe we could go in to the Art Institute or something," I said.

"I think I'll still have to be packing tomorrow," she said.

I could feel my cheeks getting red, but I was also aware that it was too dark in the car now to see this.

"All day?" I said.

She passed me the jar back. "Have to," she said.

I took a small sip of the milk. "That's cool," I said.

When I offered the jar to her this time she put up her palm and refused it. "I'm almost half used to it now."

"Huh?"

"Finish it," she said. "Go ahead."

I took one more sip of the milk, but the jar was still almost half full.

"What are you used to?" I said.

She took both her hands off the wheel and loudly cracked most of her knuckles. "Packing," she said.

"Maybe we could just go for a drive, though," I said, then gulped down the rest of the milk. "Or something like that."

"You know that I'd love to, Laughlin James. Really. You know that."

I wiped off my mouth with the back of my hand and Picasso leaned over to kiss me.

"I'm sorry," she said. "Really am. You know I would go if I could."

"Over, Under, Sideways, Down" came on the radio now. She turned it way up. "Call me," she said.

I remember that it struck me as strange that I had to go to school in the morning. "I will," I said, nodding.

We were already on the Lisle exit ramp. I was relieved that I wasn't quite all the way home yet, and at the same time I wanted to be out of the car and away from Picasso real quick.

"Or *I* can call *you* when our phone gets put in."

There was a strange slow dull ache in my cock. I just nodded.

"Should be in by next week, at the latest."

I could picture her house in Winnetka, and, in the kitchen, a new touch-tone phone on the wall, but I just could not picture Picasso.

"Or I could come up then," I said.

"Yeah, right," said Picasso.

"You know, on the train."

"Train runs right up there," she said.

She turned off the radio now, adjusted the way she was sitting, took hold of the wheel with both hands. The empty jar sat in my lap.

"Happy birthday," I said.

"Thanks," said Picasso. "And you too, L.J., in July."

"Merci," I said. "Thanks."

We drove up Main Street in silence.

"I guess we had a pretty fair time, though, you and me," she said finally. We were now on my street. "Don't you think, Laughlin James?"

"We did," I said.

"I guess that we did."

"I think so too."

"Hey, we did."

"I'll—"

Her lips touched my cheekbone, up high, and I could feel her warm breath on my eyelids.

"You sure now?" she said.

"Yes," I said. "Yes."

Rotation

I was spending my lunch hour in the Marshall Field's Men's Store, looking for a graduation present for Kevin, my youngest brother. I was twenty-four at the time (I'm twenty-nine now) so it was sometime during my second year as a Xerox account representative. The actual date of the incident I've forgotten, but I do remember that it was a Thursday on which a famous person had died; Kevin was going to graduate from high school that Saturday, the day the famous person was going to be buried . . . . Everything else about the incident I can recall very clearly.

I'd looked at a few sports shirts on the first floor before remembering that what Kevin really wanted was a tennis racquet. I hadn't planned on spending that much on his present, but since I was already inside the store I took the elevator up to the sporting goods department and had a look anyway.

The sporting goods department was the entire fifth floor of the Men's Store. It was larger than I'd expected and there was an excellent selection of tennis equipment. The racquets were displayed on revolving metal stands according to manufacturer, then subdivided by grip-size and weight. Kevin had been playing with a wooden racquet that year, and I'd heard him mention that he wanted to switch over to a steel or aluminum frame. I picked out a Wilson T-3000 4½-medium and unzipped the headcover.

After about thirty seconds a salesclerk came up and asked me if I needed any help. He was a young Oriental, very anemic looking, and with a bad case of acne. He didn't even sound as though he spoke English very well. When I said I was just looking, thank you, he moved away immediately. I took a few more abbreviated backhands with the Wilson, twisted the grip around in my palm, then put the headcover back on. I was really just killing time. But it was right around now that it first occurred to me that I might be able to take one of the racquets home with me without having to pay for it.

In those days the idea of shoplifting was still crossing my mind occasionally. I never went into a store looking to steal anything, but from time to time there were opportunities I couldn't help noticing—an unguarded calculator, for example, or even a paperback at the train station. Since these were things I could easily afford, I figured the temptation to steal them must have been a leftover teenagerly impulse to test my own nerve. Perhaps I was bored. In any event, I had only actually stolen two things, both of them while I was still going to school: from the Northwestern bookstore I'd taken a hardcover economics textbook that I honestly couldn't afford; after I'd moved out of the dorm I'd lifted a steak from the Jewel, the juices from which had leaked through the cellophane and bloodied a shirt worth five times its value. That was the extent of my shoplifting experience. Both times I'd hidden the item under my jacket then gotten in line and paid for something much less expensive; both times this method had been successful.

The plan I came up with that Thursday in Field's was quite different: I would pretend that I owned the racquet I wanted and simply walk out of the store with it.

I figured there were several advantages to this method, especially for someone like me.

(1) I looked much too respectable to be taken for a shoplifter. I had the standard businessman's haircut, did not have a beard yet, and was wearing a scarlet silk tie and a navy blue Brooks Brothers suit. I looked, in fact, like what I actually was: a rising young Xerox account rep, with no need whatever to resort to shoplifting.

(2) Tennis racquets were not likely targets for shoplifters. They were too large to conceal but not really expensive enough for a serious thief to risk getting caught over. For the same two reasons the store had neither chained them down nor encased them, nor would be guarding them all that closely. So in this sense a tennis racquet was an ideal target for me, whether my brother had wanted one or not.

(3) Because of the lunch-hour crowd, the salesclerks would be too busy to watch any one customer very carefully. All the other customers would function, then, as camouflage.

(4) If I made no effort to conceal the racquet— and I intended to dangle it about as conspicuously as possible—I wouldn't be technically guilty of stealing it until I was in the process of actually walking out the door. This was the main advantage of being in a large department store: people moved freely about them all the time with various sorts of merchandise, both the store's and their own. Once I'd made it into another department it would be almost like being in a whole other store. If anyone did question me about the racquet along the way, I could simply pretend honest confusion as to where I was supposed to have paid for it—an unlikely story, of course,

but at this point I could also produce (5) my Marshall Field's credit card and cheerfully offer to pay for whatever it was the security person refused to believe I wasn't trying to steal. That was my safety valve. Even if they knew I was lying, my businesslike appearance, plus getting paid on the spot, would probably make it easier for them to give me the benefit of the doubt, however small that doubt turned out to be.

That was the plan. I wouldn't be hiding anything and I'd act like I had nothing to hide. My biggest measure of security, then, would be the fact that I hadn't provided myself with one.

There were some problems, of course. The stairway that led from the fifth floor to the fourth was directly behind the cash registers and clearly not intended for customers (or shoplifters). The arrival and departure of the four elevators would therefore determine when I could make my initial—and most important—getaway. One's arrival would have to coincide almost exactly with when the coast had come clear; a second or two just before or just after wouldn't be good enough.

Assuming plainclothes security guards were employed, it would be impossible for me to tell who they were.

However well I was dressed, I'd still be carrying around a tennis racquet with the price tag still attached, with no bag and no receipt, so I was bound to look at least a *little* suspicious.

There was no getting around the fact that eventually I'd have to walk out a door to the street.

And if for any reason I *was* apprehended, I knew there was an excellent chance that someone at Xerox would hear about it. I'd be risking my career, then, over a tennis racquet, and one that I didn't even want all that much to begin with.

While still trying to decide whether or not to go through with it, I picked up a can of tennis balls and walked over to where the Oriental salesclerk was standing. I told him I wanted to buy the balls, and he led me to a cash register.

I paid for the balls with cash, still holding on to the T-3000. The salesclerk seemed puzzled by this but didn't say anything. He rang up the sale and put the can of balls in a bag, stapling it shut with the receipt folded across the top. I was now an official customer. The salesclerk glanced again at the T-3000 while handing me my change. Acting, then, as though I'd completely forgotten I was still holding it, I handed him the racquet and at the same time asked him whether Field's carried the Yamaha something something—I made up some model number. I added that it was similar to the Wilson T-3000 he was holding, only not quite so stiff. He handed me the bag with the balls in it and said that Field's didn't happen to carry that particular model, but in the meantime proceeded to lead me over to the display racks so we could look for one. The whole time we looked he kept repeating that the store didn't stock the Yamaha racquet I'd asked about, or, for that matter, any Yamaha racquets at all.

It was hard to say what good I thought confusing one salesclerk had done me, but as soon as this one was gone I decided to go ahead with my plan.

I walked around and looked at some of the other racquets but purposely ended up back at the Wilson display. I turned it a few times, examining it from top to bottom, then picked out another T-3000.

After procrastinating a bit, I finally started in the general direction of the elevators, trying as I moved down the aisle to take on the rhythms of a browsing lunch-hour shopper.

I stopped at the end of a row of fishing poles, just outside the imaginary semicircle within which it would have been obvious I was waiting for an elevator.

After several seconds a bell dinged and an elevator opened up, but I stayed where I was. Right away I was struck by just how much additional nerve it was going to take to get myself to actually leave the floor with the racquet.

My main task now was to remain nonchalant while picking my spot. I pretended to be looking around for help from a salesclerk, although if one had approached me, of course, the whole project would have to have been abandoned on the spot. In the meantime, in order to make myself look more like an undecided shopper, I took out and began counting the five or six bills I had in my wallet.

Another elevator opened, stood empty, then closed by itself. Again I stayed where I was. None of the salesclerks had bothered to approach me so far, and I hadn't committed myself yet, either, but already I was starting to feel less and less inconspicuous having to stand there like that with the racquet.

After missing two more opportunities, I assigned myself a firm deadline: be on one of the next three elevators or give up the project. I had good chances to make the next two, though, and both times I balked. Without even waiting for a third one, then, I went and put the T-3000 back where it belonged.

It was no small relief to be rid of it, too, but there was one bizarre catch: I was so enamored by now with the idea of having a free tennis racquet to give Kevin that I felt as though I'd just given back something I'd already paid for. The idea of buying him a racquet—or any other present, for that matter—now seemed somehow doubly uneconomical.

I rotated the Wilson display a few more times and came upon a T-2000. It was three dollars cheaper than the first racquet but the only difference seemed to be a thin metal brace two-thirds of the way up the shaft—the T-3000 had one, the T-2000 did not. Yet none of these details really mattered any more: what I wanted was a free tennis racquet. Given the way I'd just chickened out by the elevators, though, it was hard to see how I was going to get one.

At this point I had the insight of the afternoon: I would actually look *less* suspicious leaving the floor if I brought along *both* of the racquets. I picked up the T-3000 again. Someone might try to steal one tennis racquet, but they'd never try to steal two. The idea seemed so sensible that I ended up picking out a third racquet, a Donnay model with a black wooden frame. With all three headcovers up around my collar, I held the racquets in front of me like a bouquet.

I was vaguely aware that I was testing myself now, egging myself on. That was good. I could feel the blood in my hands circulating around the three shafts. . . . . At this point I added the finishing touch: three more cans of tennis balls, balanced on my forearms as awkwardly as I could manage it without dropping them.

Hugging the entire bundle against my chest, I walked directly over to the elevators and pressed the down button. I'd committed myself now once and for all. As much as I was tempted to turn around, I forced myself to keep staring ahead at the down button. I knew the alternative—craning my neck and checking in every direction—might have given me away altogether.

My adrenalin was up and I could sense that my cheeks were now flushed, but I still felt pretty sure of myself. I tried to hold back my nervousness with an air of tired impatience, of "I'm on my way to do something important now, so don't even think about bothering me." I figured that the more I could make myself believe this, the more authentic my outward expression would look.

After what seemed like a very long time, a door on my left slid open and two elderly gentlemen emerged. Without hesitating at all, I stepped past them into the elevator.

So far, so good. A young black woman had gotten in with me. She was carrying what looked to be a basketball inside a green Marshall Field's bag. Seeing the size of my own bundle, she pushed the button for the main floor for both of us. She didn't say anything; however anomalous what I was carrying must have looked to her, she seemed intent on politely minding her own business.

Right away the elevator stopped at four. The doors slid back and two six- or seven-year-old boys crowded in, followed by their mother—but by nobody else.

We stopped at three as well—I couldn't believe it—and a sixth passenger got in. All the starts and stops were making me nervous (at each floor I imagined half a dozen security guards waiting outside the door) but I also felt a lot safer backed against the wall as I was behind five other bodies.

When we stopped at two, however, I excused myself and pushed my way out. I was starting to get rattled again, especially about the part where I had to actually walk out of the store with the goods. What I needed was to postpone the moment of truth for a while and give myself a chance to get my bearings again.

The second floor was the hats and shoes department. I figured that a man carrying tennis equipment around here could have been from anywhere. I was also hoping that the little green Field's bag I was carrying would somehow help to legitimize the rest of my load. Finally, I still had the option of abandoning the whole bundle on a countertop and giving Kevin the paid-for can of balls for his graduation.

I held onto everything, though, and got ready to try my luck at the exit. Since most of the customers on this floor were using the stairway, I decided to use it myself. I also wanted to avoid running into anyone from sporting goods on the elevator.

As I reached the landing midway between the two floors, a tall, stocky middle-aged man appeared suddenly from around the corner and stood in my path. He had wavy red hair and was wearing a dark green blazer—I still can picture him clearly—and he seemed to be in a great hurry to get up the stairs. I moved to the right and looked up at him; the man stutterstepped to his left and stood in my way again. He'd said nothing so far, but I had no doubts at all that he was Field's security guard. As the man stepped back to his right, I accidentally-on purpose dropped two cans of tennis balls; the clanging echoed loudly around us in the stairwell. I started going over my alibi in a hurry now, trying to screw up some courage and, more important, some nonchalance. In the meantime the man had retrieved the two cannisters, handed them to me while muttering some apology, then sprinted off up the stairs, obviously quite disgusted by my clumsiness.

Having safely made it onto the main floor, I knew I was both better and worse off at once: I was closer now to the exits and success, but being this far from the sporting goods cash registers I was also that much more vulnerable.

I guessed that my best bet would be to appear as though I'd recently *entered* the store for as long as I could—to look, above all, like the opposite of someone about to rush off anywhere . . . . . I paused at a display of men's umbrellas and pretended to examine a few of the pricetags and handles. I also made a show of checking my watch against the huge ornate clock above the doorway, although I was so nervous by now that I doubt it even registered what the time was on either.

Twice in the next thirty seconds I browsed my way across the crowded main aisle, picking my spot. I kept my distance from the revolving doors and tried not to face them. I also tried not to think about how quickly my options were vanishing.

All of a sudden, I yawned. It was a long, drawn-out one that made my abdomen flutter. Automatically I tried to bring my hand up to cover my mouth, but I couldn't because of the load I was carrying.

It took me a second to realize—and another to appreciate—how perfect a gesture of innocence a yawn really was. Then, while I was counting my blessings, I ended up yawning again. This time I made the most of it: I put down part of my load on the plexiglass countertop and covered my mouth with my fist, drawing the whole thing out for as long as I could; in the process I managed a third yawn as well.

Fifteen feet from the exit I made one final pause. While examining a necktie with my free little finger, I stole a quick glance back down the aisle . . . . . The coast was now clear.

I let go of the tie and backed up a few paces, then turned around slowly and headed straight for the revolving brass doors. I focused my gaze on the pedestrians outside on the sidewalk. As I reached the doorway I could sense there was another person just in back of me, but I knew it was too late now to do much about it.

I leaned into the turnstile with my shoulder,

then felt the whole door turn and accelerate as this other person began to push along with me.

By now I was painfully aware that whatever alibi I came up with wouldn't be good enough, so I was rather afraid. I ended up convincing myself, in fact, that at any moment I would feel a hand on my shoulder and the jig would be up. I even decided that I would only embarrass myself by trying to make an excuse or a run for it; I would therefore admit my guilt outright and be led away quietly.

By this point I was through the second set of doors and out onto the Washington Street sidewalk. It was crowded and noisy out here, and I listened hard for the voice demanding I stop. I was neither very relieved now nor very afraid; all the uncalled-for despair in the doorway seemed to have settled my nerves.

I turned to my right and walked east. Mainly because of the sunlight's dazzle on the concrete, for the first few steps I could barely see where I was going.

The Wrong Kind of Insurance

Robert and Linda discuss the notion of the fireball rising from ground zero and sucking up buildings, the vaporization of solid material and air, their simultaneous deaths forty-six blocks from each other. It's the middle of August and hot out. They're on the East-West Tollway, headed toward Naperville, to visit Bob's son. They contrive, after paying the toll, to imagine themselves in flight from the fireball, but in the end they just can't seem to manage it.

Bob takes a cab out to Midway to make sure that Linda's new doeskin gym bag isn't still circling around on the American luggage conveyor. It isn't.

Linda absolutely agrees with Robert that it would be better to send the teaching assistants away and be by themselves, just the two of them. She squeezes Bob's biceps. He winces. Then, whispering, she admits she has no way of dealing with the two beautiful young teaching assistants. "None?" he says. "None."

A large nurse to Robert: "Fine conditioned pair of buttocks for a young man your age, I might say. Mighty fine."

Bob gets up early and prepares his own breakfast. Since the day is quite cold, he fills the stove up with wood and has a warm fire burning before leaving the house. On his way out to the garage, he notices footprints in the new-fallen snow on the lawn. The footprints, he figures, are Linda's.

They examine a pair of color photographs of atoms in motion taken by Albert V. Crewe and Michael S. Isaacson. The atoms had been magnified over eighty million times beforehand. There appear to be rather vast spaces between them. They discuss the role of model-building in scientific discovery.

Bob thinks back to the morning he'd killed two young men with a flamethrower.

The livingroom of Linda's apartment. Aside from the bathroom and cooking area, all there is to it. Dozens of trophies, hundreds of paperbacks, a Hitachi stereo system, an unfolded sofa bed, a view of nine buildings, a beige and red carpet, three maple chairs, and a table. Linda is reading *The Levels of the Game* but thinking of Navratilova. Even ten percent of $4,755,282, she thinks, is $475,528.20, is it not? She puts down the book. Is the level of Martina's tennis *ten* times higher than hers? She rolls a thin reefer and does some arithmetic and takes off her clothes. She thinks that it's not. She gets up and puts on a record. The vinyl is still in outstanding condition. The receiver is powerful, the speakers efficient. The Vandellas and Martha. And Linda, crouched on the edge of the carpet, toking the reefer, snapping her fingers, hitting an underspin backhand, and singing.

"To overrate recklessness," says Bob, "in sex or in art, it just isn't possible." Coughs. "This is so true," Linda says, "she said platitudinously, echoing Robert." Robert looks over at Linda.

Bob doffs his shirt and does twenty-four pushups. It was Linda's idea. Linda takes off her blue Fila warmup and does twenty-six pushups, for Robert. A version of foreplay, says Bob to himself, I find not uninspiring, as Linda's brisk pushups continue.

They are over at Bob's house, discussing Gretta, Bob's wife. Linda kicks off and catches then drops and picks up a navy blue Dr. Scholl's clog and fires it at the white wall. A Kline poster tilts. Bob straightens the poster, tosses the clog back, puts on his brand new tweed coat. There's a series of silences, each more discrete than the last one. When they do finally leave, Linda goes out the door quietly, first.

Bob's new office at the university overlooks a small, gardenlike park. He notices that only women appear in the park in the morning and only men in the afternoon, and that some walk alone sunk in deep meditation and that others gather in groups and engage in vehement discussions. Upon inquiring about the park, he learns from a colleague that it is annexed to a metropolitan asylum. The people in the park were inmates of the Institution, harmless patients who didn't have to be confined any more.

Robert and Linda are wrestling, and things have begun to get hairy. Linda bends back three of Bob's fingers, slaps him twice on the cheek, accidentally-on purpose scratching him with one of her nails. With his good left knee he pins her left wrist, shoving it high up her back, then tickles her hard. He's still real surprised. She cries out for mercy. He shows it. They stand, gasping for air, but not laughing. Linda grabs Bob by the shoulders and drags him down sideways. The floor starts to tremble and both receive wood burns. She snatches his neck between her taut thighs and scissors it, makes him servile to her coy disdain. His face gets all red. She crosses her ankles to get better leverage, then squeezes as hard as she can. They twist, turn, and pant. He lies and breathes on her flushed scented flesh. They keep panting.

Bob asks that Linda "only stop acting like a phage for ten seconds" and hear what he might have to say. "Yeah right," Linda says. "So I'm listening."

Linda lets Robert down easily. He goes away after saying good-bye as graciously as he could have. He grinds his real teeth, but in secret. It takes him a while to come up with the courage to be angry in public. He goes for a walk in the Loop to give himself time to think this thing over.

Jasper Johns sure looks a lot like a grouchy John Chancellor, thinks Linda. But when you squint at this photograph here, he looks like he just might start grinning.

Gradually Bob comes to realize that he's bought the wrong kind of insurance.

Bob goes out to the store and buys meat, beer, cheese, milk, grapefruit, pineapple juice, bread, straws, napkins, Merits, *People,* and raisins. Standing in line at the checkout, it comes to him, as sometimes it does, that he's nothing. When he gets back home, half a dozen gorgeous young women are waiting for him in somebody's underwear flyer. It's a little booklet, really. His mail. Standing at the divider, he has a small bowl of Wheaties with raisins. He sits down then, lights his first cigarette in four or five days, starts to read through the booklet. And he actually reads the whole thing.

Their ages do matter to them. Bob is one and a half times as old as Linda is now, to the week, and Linda is seven years older than Michael, Bob's son. Each has dark brown, medium-length hair, but Bob's hair is shorter. Bob's hair is springier, thicker. Bob teaches history of art, Linda aerobics and tennis. Linda is shorter than Bob is, but she's not much less muscular, for both are still trim and fit, for their ages.

A waiter deftly pours cognac over a souffle at the table of a corpulent couple. The woman strikes a match for the waiter. He takes it with a bow and holds it over the frying pan. The souffle flares up and the couple clap their hands. Robert and Linda look on, smoking cigarettes, utterly utterly fascinated.

It is quiet. Snow is tumbling down heavily, almost vertically, blanketing the sidewalk and street. There are no passersby. The dreary streetlights are flickering uselessly. Linda runs two hundred steps to the corner and stops for a moment. Three men are after her, hurrying, closing the gap left between them.

Gretta to Bob now: "You take it so lightly. Do you even remember that there once was a closeness between us that may have been based on the fact of our being man and wife but actually went far beyond it?" There isn't a single thing Bob can think of to say to her.

Bob wakes up in a strange hotel bed, on the coast. He smells airplanes and hay, and feels nauseous. His room phone is ringing. It's 5:17 in the morning. It's Linda, who's joyous. She's taken up painting. They discuss this decision. Since his phone is tied up, Bob can't order coffee or pineapple juice. He shivers and blinks and keeps talking.

Linda opens her mailbox, finds only junk mail inside. No first-class stamps or even handwriting, except perhaps for the imitation script used in advertising circulars, certainly no letter from Robert. She crumples the thin sheaf of papers, uncrumples it, then tears it all up, showering it neatly into her lobby's brass wastebasket. Curses.

Robert's old mouth, which is used to talking too much, is exhausted. He is thinking of Gretta, of Michael. His class is impatient. At last his mouth speaks: of Kline, of China, of brushwork, and what it is saying makes sense. Makes other things make sense as well. Bob can now tell that his pons is intact, in spite of his madness for Linda.

Linda is nervous. She wishes she did not have to write the three-page instruction manual on How to Teach Doubles to Singles, even though Bob the Professor has promised to help her. She sits at the table, picks up her pencil, then springs back up right away, as though scalded.

Clogs, Bob decides, make Linda's sweet calves look superb.

It's six oh oh something something, thinks Robert, trying to come up with a zip code. He's just received tenure. He's joyous. While he riffles through a drawerful of envelopes, an attractive young teaching assistant comes into his office, carrying with her the cover, just the cover, of the new Scissors Kick 45.

Young Linda helpless, on tiptoe. It is midnight. The rain

is beating hard on the windows. Robert's caressing her knees, on his own, taking his God damn sweet time, very lightly.

Two Thomasville coordinated bookcase units, featuring sixteen-inch-deep adjustable shelves with matching pecan veneers, are purchased, for $358, by Linda.

Bob's note to Linda: "This is just to say I have eaten the Oreos and yogurt you were probably saving for breakfast. Delicious. Forgive me. Delicious."

Drunk, the both of them, at a jammed U. of C. New Year's Eve party, one of the two that they go to, by taxi. "Perhaps we should call this an enterprise," says Robert, "of some sort." There's a whoop. "You're just drunk," Linda says. There's a belch, from behind them. Another. "I'm drunker." Opening chord, "Cowgirl in the Sand," volume on 8¼, surprising like lightning and thunder. It's a chord neither's heard in ten years, maybe longer. "Or, you know," shouts Bob, "a symposer."

Morning. The low clouds of fall. Lots of wind. Then, the sun. Tough city pigeons refuse to give ground or scatter as Robert and Linda rush past the dumb orange Calder. The sun disappears. Their court date's in seventeen minutes. The sun comes back out. They keep walking.

Unclothed Singularities

The man tells the woman that lately she looks a lot thinner.

They play a video game having as its object the vaporization of enemy forces, but never their torture.

The man, out of nowhere, touches the woman's throat with his nose, and they shiver.

It's winter, so it keeps getting darker and colder.

The man's attractiveness to the woman has to do with the subconscious terms in which she once had to deal with her father.

They receive, after waiting six minutes, three badly cropped and lit color photographs of themselves, for a dollar.

The woman will cherish these photographs, not, as one might have thought, for a very short time, but forever.

They listen to snatches of a blues for the turn of the millenium improvised on the spot by a blind black old harp player.

The man tells the woman a joke about sucrose polyester.

They listen to the Buzzcocks' version of "Sister."

The woman reaches into her purse and discovers a two-day-old transfer.

Each gives his order, in French, to the waiter.

The man tells the woman a joke about soccer.

The man begins to gesticulate like a mother.

The woman examines the man's torso's shape, through his sweater.

Neither smokes after dinner because neither one is on fire.

The berserk young optionsmonger breaks into the woman's apartment and steals every last one of her blankets.

Accidentally-on-purpose, with the side of her wrist, the woman brushes the man's wool-clad buttocks.

They discuss the advantages of left-handedness in baseball and racquet sports.

The woman tells the man that, just the other day, she'd seen an air conditioner sticking out of somebody's window with six inches of snow piled on top of it.

The woman wants to walk right up to the man and give him a great big kiss, Mmwah!

The woman avers having once met the man's two assistants.

They walk fourteen blocks in the cold to get to a popular watering hole, then book without drinking.

They assume the Original Position.

The woman offers a fatal counter-example to something the man has just posited.

The woman casually mentions that her landlord's been getting kind of stingy with the heat these last nights.

The man attempts the use of the *sextuple entendre*.

The man gathers that his pronunciation of a movie star's name was just lethally humorous.

The man's sense of timing, he thinks, is just wicked.

They take a cab crosstown to the woman's apartment.

By word of mouth, barely, they tend to communicate.

Both remain potential cases of Spontaneous Human Combustion.

With them, information theory tends to go by the boards.

To them, Chicago remains *the* most American city.

The man sometimes feels as though the top of his head's flying off in all these crazy new directions at once.

Is this thing just another one of those one-shot deals? one of them wonders.

First come, first served, one of them thinks.

It takes two to tango, they know.

With laughable ease, the woman resists the temptation to play the shameless hussy.

The woman does own a teeshirt that says MAKE ME LATE FOR BREAKFAST in bold purple letters, but she never has worn it in public.

They tentatively agree that the *Grosse Fuge* is, you know, better than it sounds.

St. Lucia, Queen of Light, pray for us.

Their respective careers become the topic of alternatingly sincere and ironical conversation.

Because, okay, the thing of it is, about this woman you know? the man's kinda warm for her form.

The woman gets one of these weird little sexual brain-cramps.

The man grabs a glance at the woman's still clothed singularities.

Naked men, we think, naked women.

They listen and dance to "Radio, Radio."

They listen and dance to "The Breaks."

They breathe hard and dance hard and sweat.

The woman performs six *flexiones*.

They sweat, pant, and groan.

They wrestle so vigorously the floor starts to tremble.

They both receive wood burns.

The man examines all the little doodads and things in the woman's strange bathroom.

They discuss the poised SS-20s, the new video mastering processes, lust, sweat, Johns, Bosch, Haig, Grass, Trojan Horse, Curtis Blow, Demerol hydrochloride, flash-to-bang time, inexpensive imitation 1952 Fender Telecasters, the weather, the dance, the novel, the drama, the blues.

They collapse into bed.

Certain lengths to which neither are prepared to go in order to facilitate innovative sexual intercourse between consenting adults remain unascertained.

They fail to notice the absence of blankets.

Neither smokes, so, upon making love, neither does.

Instead, still in bed, they shiver together till morning, together, till the sun comes back up and the heat comes back on, in the morning.

Ante Meridiem

Linda Hadley turns on her side away from the light through the curtains, shivers, presses her elbows against herself. The digital clock on the night table flicks ahead to 6:46. Linda stares at the rocker three feet away from the bed, closes her eyes again, winces.

She opens her eyes and just lies there.

The bedroom is large—fifteen by twelve, plus an east-facing alcove off one of the short walls—and contains the night table, the rocker, two mahogany dressers, a fig tree planted in an old wooden tub in the alcove, a stack of five crates full of albums, a headless male mannequin, three small bookcases crammed with paperback novels and plays, the queen-sized brass bed. The walls, trim, bookshelves, and ceiling are painted flat white.

Linda pushes the sheet and blanket back off her legs and gets out of bed in one motion. She's wearing a faded green teeshirt, three or four sizes too large, with BMW printed across the front in blue letters; on the back it says SIOUX CITY CYCLES. She moans now and stretches elaborately as the day's rising light filters in.

A framed poster hangs over each of the dressers: *Untitled Number Seven* by Richard Lindner, and the Graham Gallery's reproduction of Alice Neel's *Florio*. To the left of the alcove is a five-foot-high canvas in which a woman stands nude in sidelong view to a mirror, looking down, and is drying her hair with a towel; the mirror shows only the towel. To the right of the alcove is a trophy of nine-pointed antlers.

Linda moves now, still stiff, to the rocker and picks up the blue jeans she'd draped over one of the arms five and a half hours before. Thumbprints of green and white paint are smeared across the pockets in back. She reaches into one of these pockets, takes out a key and a quarter, weighs them on her palm for a second, stares at them, drops them back in.

In his room down the hall, Will Watson Hadley's still sleeping. A battered beige Fender Jazzmaster lies halfway out of its case on the floor with the clothes Will has worn for the last two or three days strewn around it. There's also a left-handed first baseman's glove, a green nylon backpack, a safe, a six-colored cube, a Vox practice amp, eight or ten albums, their covers, and two electronic math quizzers, all part of the general chaos. A poster of Keith Richard grimacing, hitting a bar chord, is taped to one wall by three of its corners; the fourth is curling back down over his hair. The network of dark gorged veins in his forearm stands out and glistens with sweat.

Linda opens the door and comes in.

"Won'tie."

Will stirs.

She pulls her hair back off her forehead and sits on the side of the bed. "Come on now, honey. It's time."

No response.

She touches his hip through the covers. "Let's go now."

Will groans and turns over, exposing a taut little shoulder and biceps. He just has turned nine.

Linda watches him lie there a while, running her hand down his side, then gets up off the bed. "Let's go, Won'tie. Time to get up and pee for me now."

Long silence.

"Hey Mom?" says Will finally. He's stretching now, yawning, but his eyes are still closed.

"Mm?"

"Which one of those animal's named, you know, after a Mazda?"

She can see that he's still half asleep. "I think it's a kudu," she says. "Or maybe an onyx perhaps."

He opens his eyes, blinks, stares past her shoulder. "Is there my school today too?"

"*Oh* yeah," she says. "Afraid so."

"Or a kudu or something like that?"

She looks down now at his clothes, her glove, the guitar. "Or something like that."

Will nods.

"You up now?" she says.

Will just nods.

She rinses her mouth and her toothbrush then examines her face in the mirror in three-quarters profile, tracing the line of her cheek with her thumb as she moves her whole torso and head toward and away from the image, winking, squinting, raising her chin, glancing sideways, changing but slightly the cast of the fluorescent light on her face but never the angle of profile.

She starts a kettle on top of the stove then sits at the small kitchen table. Spread out before her are two vials of insulin, a half-cc 100-unit syringe still in its orange and gray paper wrapper, an apple, a light blue delft filled with cat's eyes, a Q-tip, a bottle of alcohol. She dips the Q-tip into the alcohol, swabs the top of both vials, then tears the wrapper off the syringe and twists the gray plastic sheath off the needle. Concentrating now, yawning hugely, she aerates both vials by withdrawing the syringe's gray plunger, sticking the needle in through the vials' pink rubber membranes, and forcing the plunger back down: fifteen units of air in the Lente, six in the Regular. The kettle starts whistling. Leaving the needle inside the upside down Regular vial, she draws out twenty-five units of insulin. Then, holding the transparent cylinder up to the light from the window, gripping it tightly, she snaps it three times with her fingernail, hard, and two times again even harder, dislodging two small bubbles of air from the sides and forcing them up to the top. She hears Will's voice from the hallway—"Hey Mom . . ."—but ignores it. "Hey *Mom.*" She tilts the syringe about twenty degrees and snaps it again, driving the bubbles together and centering them under the needle as one, then forces it upward and out into the Regular vial by pushing the plunger to 6. The kettle now shrieks in full cry. Upending the Lente, she pushes the needle in, changes grip, slowly draws the plunger back down to 21 and leaves it right there, double-checking its final position. Then she lifts off the vial, fits the sheath back on over the needle, breathes out, and blinks. The kettle continues to whistle.

Will, dressed now, finishes tying his track shoes. The unstuck corner of the Richard poster above him billows and falls a half inch or so in the warm rising air from the radiator. Will reaches into his pocket, takes out some change—mostly nickels—and begins to examine it carefully, mumbling, whispering, figuring out loud to himself how much he's worth.

Using a gram scale, Linda weighs out sixty-five grams of banana, thirty of Wheaties, two hundred of two-percent milk.

Will strolls into the kitchen. "Bwana Anna's up, Mom. She's got hiccups I think."

"Okay," says Linda. "I know." She pulls two teabags from a gray china pot and wrings them between their strings and a teaspoon. "Good morning."

"Morning."

Will moves past her now to the window.

"Wheaties all right for breakfast?"

He touches the pane with his forehead. "Or how about . . ."

"How about Wheaties."

Will stares out past Stuyvesant Town at their six-degree view of the river. "There goes one of those boats," he says. "Look."

She goes to the window and looks out over his head. The boat's disappeared.

Will switches on the TV. "Or but how about French toast or something."

She carries his cereal bowl and his glass to the table. "We're all out of eggs, so I'm letting you have extra milk."

Will changes channels—commercial, commercial, Diane Sawyer, commercial—then settles for some old cartoon.

"The banana's your juice," says Linda. "Did you pee for a second time yet?"

Will just stares at the set.

"Won'tie."

He does not turn around. "Can't yet," he says.

"I know," says Linda. "But still go and try though, okay? We don't need a gallon, you know." She lowers the TV set's volume, watches for five or six seconds, then turns off the set altogether. "You go and pee in the catcher and I'll go get Bwana."

Anna, thirteen months old, whines, kicks, and hiccups while Linda strips off her old Pamper.

74

"That's one king-sized fume, m'dear," says Linda. "Let me tell you."

There's a small oil portrait of Will—wide-eyed, looking surprised about something—hanging, slightly crooked, on the wall to the left of the crib. It hasn't been framed yet.

"Let me tell you," says Linda.

Changed, Anna sits herself up, presses her nose to her ankle, and belches.

Sideways now on his chair in the kitchen, Will's humming Who riffs and counting his money again. His jeans are rolled down past his knees.

Linda comes in with Anna. She squeezes between Will and the counter and slides Anna into her high chair. "Pee again yet?"

"Yup."

"That's my guy."

Anna starts crying.

Linda opens a cup of strawberry yogurt, stirs up the fruit from the bottom, brings yogurt and teaspoon to Anna.

"Hey Mom . . ."

"What."

Will stares at Anna as Linda dips the unused end of the Q-Tip into the bottle of alcohol, picks up the loaded syringe, and twists off the sheath with her teeth. He is silent.

"Left leg or right leg this morning?"

Will thinks. He touches his left arm, his right arm, and then his right thigh, following what's apparently a regular pattern, thinking hard.

Linda waits.

"This one," he says, patting his upper left thigh. "Think it's this one."

She kneels on the floor between his leg and the table. "You sure now?"

Will frowns and nods.

"Think so too."

Will glances down at the needle.

Linda swabs a square inch or so of his thigh, takes the sheath from her teeth and tosses it onto the table, then pinches together a small ridge of flesh. "Hungry?" she says.

"Kinda," says Will. He affects a Cockney accent as Linda changes hands with the syringe and poises it over the spot she's just swabbed. "I will confess to a certain hungriness, yes."

Inserting the needle with one hand, Linda uses the other to draw back the plunger, checking for blood, and then to reverse the plunger's direction and force in the twenty-one units of insulin.

Will stares down blankly as the needle comes out.

"Eat up now, kiddo," says Linda. She wipes away with the Q-Tip the droplet of insulin that's oozing up out of the puncture. "Okay?"

Anna points and says, "Hot."

"Really good show, Mom," says Will. "For a junkie's old lady." He tugs up his jeans. "I mean, that was bloody well done."

Linda gets up off the floor. She bends back the needle, gathers together sheath, syringe, wrapper, and Q-Tip, then dumps them all into the garbage pail.

Without touching any part of it with her fingers, she shakes a single Clinitest tablet out of its bottle and into the upside down cap. Then she draws several drops of Will's urine from the green plastic receptacle he's left on top of the toilet and carefully squeezes two of the drops back out into a test tube.

She fills a second dropper under the faucet and dilutes the two drops of urine with ten drops of water, silently counting each of the drops to herself. Then she upends the Clinitest tablet into the clear yellow liquid.

Holding the top of the test tube with one hand, she screws the cap back onto the Clinitest bottle, pours the rest of Will's urine into the toilet, flushes it down, and rinses the receptacle out in the sink with the other—all this while watching the solution continue to boil and fizz, bubbling up toward her fingers, changing color from dark blue to dark green to green, and finally settling back down into the bottom half inch of the test tube, an inert milky beige much much much too hot to touch.

An empty milk carton, launched by the side of Will's foot, caroms off the bottom panel of the refrigerator then off two cabinet doors, bounces between table and chair legs, spins around several times on one of its corners, and stops. Anna's enthralled and dismayed. Her yogurt cup, disemboweled, lies on its side on the floor.

Linda comes into the kitchen. "Come on now, Won'tie. Relax."

Will kicks the carton again. It ricochets crazily off the windowsill, skids back along the stove and the countertop, and grazes the plexiglass door of the toaster oven, popping it open.

"God damn it, Will. Now sit down and eat."

The telephone rings.

"Will, I mean it."

Will kicks the carton one final time, not very hard, then goes and sits down in his chair. "What was I," he says, pulling himself ceremoniously up to the table. "Was I blue?"

The phone rings a second time, and Anna says something like *kick*.

Linda picks up the phone. To Will she says, "Brown. Just hurry up now and finish and then go and brush."

"You mean, one?"

"Hello," she says, into the phone. "Hi." She nods yes at Will and holds up her index finger. "Right . . . no, no . . . no. Not really . . . right. Just . . . right. The usual antics and all."

"Is that Gordon?" says Will.

"Chocolate wine, eh," she says. She looks down at Anna. "Right . . . yeah . . . but tres declasse with that dinner . . . Exactly. Though . . . no . . . no . . . not really. More like a modified limited hunger strike . . . right. How it is."

She's spotted the yogurt by now; it had been hidden before by the table. "Shit . . . no no no . . . nothing."

"Is that Auntie Miriam?"

She kneels by the high chair and shakes her head no, then begins spooning what's left of the yogurt back into the cup. "Before . . . yeah, but before . . . right. His school has only half day today . . . right."

She moves back and forth between faucet and floor, stretching the phone cord, sponging up the rest of the yogurt and rinsing it out in the sink. "So I'd have to be . . . yeah. Or she just doesn't have all the dots on her dice . . . You know, what you do to a . . . yeah, to a clutch . . . Exactly. And I'll have to be home here then anyway . . . right. For his lunch."

Still rinsing and listening, using the tip of her ring finger, she samples a fragment of strawberry.

"Yeah, but it's really that *other* type of destruction I'm hoping for . . . I hope so . . . nope . . . nope. *Or* the Pope . . . You got it . . . I guess so . . . and pretty soon they'll be recruiting *you* for the Insane Unknowns too."

"I need some more money," says Will. "That stuff costs a dollar."

"Exactly," says Linda. "These things happen, I guess, here in Hadleyville."

"I need some more money," says Will.

Linda peels another banana and brings the top third to Anna. "*Oh* yeah," she says. "It's still always there, but we just don't go to it any more."

She stands behind Will in the doorway, straightening his collar, adjusting the straps of his backpack.

"All right, Mom. All *right*. But so what's the twenty-five plus the, you know, eighty-six?"

"A dollar is plenty, kiddo. A dollar eleven. That's plenty."

"A dollar eleven?"

"That's plenty. And please don't forget."

Will turns around, doesn't say anything.

"Okay? Your ten-o'clock snack's in your backpack."

"Mommy, I won't. Jeez."

"Just hold still."

"So can Gordon come over?"

She zips up his jacket. "We'll see."

"I mean, for lunch."

"Although you're not doing nothing with nobody till that pigsty of yours gets cleaned up."

"You know, after school."

"I'll call up his father and ask him. But I'm serious, Will."

"So but can he?"

"I'll talk to Mr. Boyle about it. I'll see you at lunchtime."

She holds the door open for him, and they kiss.

"So long now."

"Okay."

Will goes out.

"And just make sure you cross at the crossing this time."

She closes the door.

She opens the door, leans out, and calls down the hallway: "Don't forget now, Won'tie. Bye bye."

Gingerly, using two napkins, she lifts a mousetrap and mouse out from under the sink in the kitchen.

She drops the whole package onto the center of the sheet from the *Times* she'd spread out before on the floor.

She stares at the mouse for a while, on her hands and her knees, then rotates the paper and starts rereading one of the stories.

She shampoos her hair, scrubs her neck and her face with a loofa sponge, then washes her shoulders, abdomen, armpits, and in back of her ears with a facecloth. She's humming. Anna's just outside the shower curtain, supporting herself with the radiator while she tries to stand up.

In a singsong voice, while rinsing her hair, Linda calls out: "Bwana *Anna* . . . Oh where *are* you?" Her eyes are shut tight.

The mirror is clouded with steam. A chrome and black electric razor, unplugged and sweating, sits on the sink counter alongside Will's urine receptacle, her hairbrush, some scissors. The wilted top third of a Puff protrudes from the top of its box.

Linda props her heel on the side of the tub and starts shaving her ankles and calves. "Bwana *Anna* . . ." The shower beats down on her back. "Oh where *are* you?"

Anna's dragged the stack of Linda's clean folded clothes off the radiator and is spreading them out on the floor.

"Bwana *Had*ley . . ."

Anna pulls herself up now by the seat of the toilet, turns and looks back at the shower curtain, then lets Linda's best pair of bluebell silk panties slide down into the water.

Linda sips her cold tea, grimaces, puts down the cup on her dresser. She's now wearing a green flannel shirt, the blue jeans, white sweat socks, and black and white sneakers. She rubs her wet hair with a towel.

"Bwana *Anna* . . ."

She rolls a feltless gray tennis ball in Anna's direction. Woefully failing to field it, Anna turns on her palms and crawls after it.

"Really good catch there, girl," says Linda. "I mean, that was a really nice catch."

"But very unfancy," she says, on the phone again now in the kitchen. "Right . . . right . . . right. So I heard."

She fingers a wet lock of hair, pulling it straight, twisting it in either direction. The kettle starts whistling.

"Poor him," she says. "But not even for B cents worth of postage apparently."

She drops two fresh teabags into the pot, laughs out loud at something the caller has said, pours in hot water. Anna stands up and starts whining.

"Apparently not . . . right. And we both gotta

book . . . definitely . . . but the word, I think, is unmod-
ulated."

She takes an apple from a basket on top of the
refrigerator, runs it under cold water, then slices off a
very small wedge. She does her best to get Anna to take it.
"So we'll be counting on . . . hope not . . . I hope not."

Holding the phone and the apple wedge, lean-
ing way over to clasp Anna's hand, she does a little jig by
the sink.

"So listen . . . I'll see you . . . I'll be . . . all right
then . . . okay now . . . bye bye."

On out into the diningroom finally, carrying Anna, the
apple, a Pamper. She turns on the radio and lays Anna
down on the carpet.

The news has to do with the non-military
ramifications of the flight of the spaceship *Columbia*.
Linda takes a bite of the apple, listens, strips off Anna's
used Pamper.

The radio sits at the end of a long polished
cedar chest; besides the single captain's chair, the table,
and a desktop-sized Xerox machine on the floor, it's the
room's only furniture. Seven bookshelves, all empty, are
recessed into the wall by the fireplace. Most of the plas-
terboard on the other three walls is exposed, and paint-
spattered dropcloths are bunched in the corners. It's
dusty.

"You just went, what?" says Linda. "Twenty
minutes ago?" She squeezes Anna's belly and tickles her.
"Didn't you, you litle turd. *Didn*'t you."

Anna squirms, twists, and shrieks.

"You're just my great big little shitter now,
aren't you?" She fastens the adhesive tape stays. "Aren't
you, you little flesh-colored turd?"

Anna sneezes.

"Bless you," says Linda.

Anna sneezes again, and again.

"Why bless you!" says Linda.

Anna starts laughing.

Linda goes back into the kitchen now, dumps the used Pamper into the garbage pail and picks up her teacup, unplugs the telephone, comes back out to the diningroom.

She sits at the table. Spread out before her are the apple and teacup, a circular mirror propped up by art books and atlases, a second blue delft full of rose petals, pencils, sketch paper, brushes, a sponge, a neat stack of postcards, dozens of tubes of acrylics, a six-foot-square rectangular canvas, a pad of white palette paper.

Linda stares down at Anna. "Seen and Not Seen" comes on the radio now. Linda coughs.

Anna's hunched on the carpet, leaning forward, coloring on one of Will's old alphabet blocks with a craypa.

Linda flexes the cords in her neck for a second, stares at the mirror, relaxes.

The canvas shows what is apparently Linda— although at this stage the eyes in the painting are gray, almost black, whereas Linda's are medium green, the color of spring praying mantes—facing left in three-quarters profile; a small naked child, its buttocks supported by the mother's right forearm, rests its head, facing left, on the mother's right shoulder.

Linda squeezes out two lines of acrylic onto the used palette sheet. Inhaling its odor, using a No. 6 red sable brush, she starts mixing a small dab of titanium white with some carmine.

She stops.

Headlong glance at the mirror, the canvas: she thinks that she's not very good, and it bothers her.

Anna throws down the block and starts clapping.

Linda takes up some white with a second, smaller-gauged brush, stares at the mirror, squints, sips her tea. Motes of dust, old ash, and plaster drift through the wide shaft of sunlight around her.

She raises her brush to the canvas and looks at the delft.

"Now where was I," she says, to herself.

Roque Dalton García
Is Dead

Linda opens her legs and starts soaping her
labia, singing to herself about nothing, as is her custom, in
melodic perfecto contralto. She scrubs her flushed face
with a washcloth, then lathers her abdomen, her breasts,
and her armpits. She scrubs and shaves and daydreams
and sings. She shampoos her hair, takes a brush to her
back and her feet, rinses herself thoroughly off.

Clean again, she stops singing and gets out of
the shower. Two young men are waiting for her in the
bathroom. One hands her a towel, the second puts an
Ingram MAC-10 to her temple and tells her to put up her
hands, that she's under arrest.

"For what?" says Linda, raising one hand.

"For the murder of José Guillermo García,
Joaquin Villalobos, José Antonio Morales Carbonel, Pilar
Ternera, Roque Dalton García, Vasco 'Duende' Gon-
calves, Alvaro Magaña, and José Rodofo Viera," says the
man with the gun. "And so put down that towel already."

"But Dalton García is already dead," says
Linda. "I'm clean."

There's a silence.

"We know that," says the man with the gun.

Linda is dripping, gooseflesh has risen, she
shivers. Both of her hands are now raised, the towel is
now on the floor. There isn't a single thing she can think of

to say to these guys. That she might sing for them, well, this isn't even considered.

The man who'd handed Linda the towel to begin with now slaps her across the face, twice, first with the back of his hand, then with the front, very hard.

"We already, know that!" he says.

The Skinner

For a second offense, Bernadette's sentence is light. It's only The Skinner. To help prevent backlogs, such sentences are executed immediately. Bernadette removes all her clothing and enters The Skinner without having to be dragged, then lies down by herself on the smooth aluminum table, facing up. The door closes behind her, out go the lights.

Right away she is frozen electrically into a spread-eagled position. Not one muscle can move. Two surgical blades begin moving upward from the tip of each middle toe, slicing through Bernadette's skin at a depth of exactly two-seventeenths of an inch. The Skinner does not make mistakes. At the same time, a third blade begins where the first two will eventually stop, a point midway between Bernadette's two lowest ribs and her navel. This blade moves up her chest, throat and face, automatically following with sonar Bernadette's personal topography, and ends by parting her scalp to the rear of her cranium. In the meantime, blades four and five are working their way down from the tip of each middle finger toward either end of her collarbone, where they'll head for her throat.

Next, twenty-six pincers (they are not unlike alligator clips) fasten themselves at regular intervals along both sides of the five seams of skin and begin parting it. The pincers are programmed to peel the skin back quickly but carefully, so as to cause neither undue suffering nor rips.

Despite these precautions, Bernadette is now in some pain, so a syringe is raised from the table and a small dose of morphine is administered into the base of her spine. Since speech is impossible for one being skinned, The Skinner itself must determine both the drug and the dosage, as well as if and when a painkiller is necessary to begin with—but not once has it failed to do so correctly. About two quarts of Bernadette's blood have also been lost, so a transfusion of plasma is given. Again, the required amount is determined remotely by The Skinner's own delicate sensors.

Once her skin's been removed, the current is turned off and Bernadette is helped from the table. Two nurses apply a special petroleum salve, in order to prevent further blood loss or shock, then help her get dressed. The Skinner prints out a prescription for Darvocet and codeine to relieve the normal discomfort once the morphine wears off. It also suggests that Bernadette wear all-cotton clothing for eight to ten months.

Fully convinced now not to do any more of whatever it was she was doing before she was sentenced, Bernadette is free to go home to her family, to grow a new skin, eventually to return to her job—and to start, it is hoped, an entire new life for herself

The Eye of Hunan

Hunan, Kham Ping's young son, is knelt in the gravel before her. It is announced he is guilty of attending a school in the city. Using the legs of his great-great-grandmother's table, three Khmer Rouge soldiers begin clubbing Hunan to the ground. Kham Ping is restrained by two others.

During the beating, Hunan's left eye somehow pops out. Noticing this, one of the soldiers calls for a halt to the blows and kneels by the body. She picks Hunan's eye from out of the gore, rolls it around on her palm, then deftly tosses it up to Kham Ping—who, in her daze, accidentally-on purpose manages to catch it.

Inside her hand, what's left of the eye does not proceed to sprout wings and soar heavenward. It teaches no one in the city to see, for it cannot see itself. It does not reveal to Kham Ping any secrets. Nor does it disintegrate into a vapor, scalding the hand of its mother. It does not teach the soldiers a lesson.

For two days Kham Ping wanders the deserted streets of the city, clutching the eye of her son.

Torque

Tuesday, and I'm in The Gap again, hawking straightlegged Levi's and smoking the last cigarette of my life: my pack of Old Golds is now empty, and I've vowed never to buy another one. An attractive young woman is in one of the dressing rooms, trying on a pair of my pants, and I'm watching her through one of the three two-way mirrors in the office, passing the time while I wait for the manager. I'm also listening to Brubeck and Mulligan *Live at the Berlin Philharmonic* on the tape deck. The manager will be back any minute with his own pack of cigarettes, so this will be my first big chance to test my resolve.

Unhappy with the first pair she tries on, the woman begins pushing the stiff denim jeans back down over her thighs. As I watch her struggling out of them, I fall somehow into a kind of half-lucid reverie: I imagine that the fate of the planet's four billion people hangs on whether I can toss the empty pack of Old Golds into the wastebasket. The wastebasket is next to the doorway, about eight feet away; although the edge of the manager's desk blocks my view of half of the rim, the toss is quite makeable. It has to be me who makes this toss, it has to be made from where I'm already standing, and it has to be done *on the first try*. All the rules governing the toss, it seems, have been specified by "a U.N. committee assembled especially for the occasion." I'll be forced, for example, to stand behind a thin purple line in the blue carpet's pattern which is being monitored by a beam of light; if broken by my shoe, the light's circuit will automatically trigger the destruct mechanism. If I miss the same thing will happen: the entire planet will start falling apart a continent at a time, according to alphabetical order, then explode into space. Africa, I realize, would be the first land-mass to go, then, though not by that much.

Across the polarized glass from me, the woman is casually testing the elastic in her panties and fiddling with a thin silver chain she wears looped twice around her waist (and from which, I notice, nothing is hanging). She appears through for the moment with the trying-on process, but not about to go anywhere or get dressed again, either. The toss, I decide, will be dedicated to her.

I am ready, sweaty palms and all. At my imagined request, "The Sermon on the Mount" has become the designated background music. My second request, though, for one final cigarette, has been denied by the committee.

Weighing the pack in my palm, I find it heavy and well-balanced enough to be accurate with. Everything is set.

I breathe deeply and toss as I exhale, thinking, All the good luck in the world can't save it now . . .

From the beginning it looks like a basket. The pack, however, manages to graze the edge of the desk top, then caroms about thirty degrees off its arc and falls out of sight . . .

But the committee sees everything; they have the whole toss on videotape and will need only a second or two to issue their findings.

When I look back in on her now, the woman appears to be staring straight into my eyes. Her sweater is pulled up and she has both breasts cupped in her hands, kneading them like bread dough while tweaking herself on the nipples. Instinctively I lower my gaze and hold in my stomach.

The committee's findings are that my toss hadn't been as accurate as they'd hoped, but that gravity had helped force the pack back on course; special Earth-resources technology satellites tracking its flight had determined that wind resistance was also a factor as the pack had begun to uncrumple. All this can be seen in the committee's slow motion replay. In the end the pack had been able, the desk top notwithstanding, to just catch the far inside of the rim of the wastebasket, poise there for a second, then topple back into it.

The manager of The Gap returns to his office at exactly this moment.

North America

Beryl peeled a banana and found two short curly hairs inside, sprouting sideways out of the fruit like two houseplants, like a pair of hideous S's. But she didn't tell *any*one, not even Tracy, her brown-haired twin sister who was sitting right next to her. She simply dumped the banana and continued solving her math problems.

Four days later it happened again, once again inside a Chiquita. This time Beryl showed Tracy the two little hairs—how they were sticking up from between the fruit and the peel like stretched-out square-root signs. Both girls thought in terms of vomiting furiously. But how had two pubic hairs twice found their way inside an unpeeled banana? they wanted to know. Why did pubic hairs have to be so springy and yukky all the time, anyhow? If they took this stuff to a show-and-tell session at school, would the other kids accuse them of planting the hairs? And how gross this all was! Could God have accidentally-on purpose allowed pubic hairs to grow inside some bananas?

Being from suburban North America, Beryl and Tracy were unable to understand the mysterious, much less put up with it. They each aggressively peeled another Chiquita, but found only banana. Satisfied immensely, out of bananas, they sighed and returned once again to their bourgeois, free-market homework—just in time, too, for their businesslike, heterosexual father to enter the room and smile down at them.

Young Seventh-World
Women

One Wednesday evening, in the middle of "Starsky and Hutch," a small group of young seventh-world women knocks on my door. There are six of them, their perfect skins range from dark ocher to beige, and I am impressed. Once inside they begin removing their bizarre looking costumes—all very deliberately, too, an article at a time, each, I can tell, showing off for me as well as for the others. I'm unable to stop them. Stripped down completely, then, they march as a unit into my living room, their exquisite seventh-world jewelry glistening in the bulblight.

To be on the safe side I examine their passports and take each of their fingerprints, asking them to have a seat while I run off some copies. I also bring in three extra chairs and pass around two boxes of mints to help keep them occupied.

When I return to the living room, I introduce myself and ask the women why they are here—naked, this far from home, and all sitting crammed so tightly together on my living room couch.

Five "didn't know" and the sixth is obviously lying when she says she was prospecting for feldspar deposits in the neighborhood and "just decided" to drop by.

To break this impasse, one of them suggests that we try some friendly tag-team wrestling, them against me. I think about this for a second, then cautiously accept. As soon as I do they're upon me.

Two incredible hours go by.

Finally it's midnight. One by one, the women begin to get up, make some excuse, and start getting dressed. I personally show each to the door; each thanks me for my hospitality and gives me a light peck on the cheek. Not one of them will actually leave, though, until I've firmly stamped her passport and handed over all four copies of her fingerprints.

"But how," I ask one, "did you know that I'd only made four?"

"Special Earth-resources technology satellites," she says. "How else could one know?"

She's out the door and down the stairs before I can get a straight answer. I decide to forget about it.

At last only one of the women remains. Naturally I assume she'll be wanting *her* documents, too, so I go off to my safe to retrieve them. But when I get back she is gone.

All that's left is her national costume lying in a heap on the floor: a single piece of teal-blue silk, three mauve polyester scarves, some unexceptional panties, and a pair of silver high heels. I can't help picturing her now, either, walking by herself in the dark without this national costume, and I rush out into the night to return it.

All six women, however, are waiting for me downstairs in the lobby. They're now wearing identical maroon kneesocks and plaid skirts and blazers, brandishing pistols with silencers, and laughing hysterically. One of them produces a white plastic handcuff, and they place me "under arrest."

In silence now, they lead me outside, where a huge limousine is double-parked with all of its doors open. I also notice that none of the street lights seems to be working.

"Where are we headed?" I ask, and the handcuff behind me is only drawn tighter.

The Venturi Effect

Wind plus all the architecture was causing hundreds of small artificial tornadoes to hover around the Picasso. Suddenly one whipped Patrick backwards, sideways, and down, flat on his back. A curse reached his tongue, but he stood up and swallowed it. Then everything went back to normal. He proceeded east on Washington Street, already four minutes late for his lunch date with Sylvia.

Two blocks later Patrick imagined: a Dominican priest shares their table with them (no booths are available) and picks up the check, using a green and brown credit card. Patrick runs out of cigarettes and everything's very mixed up. After dessert, the priest mentions (twice) the gospel according to Matthew—his "personal favorite"—and complains about "tar." Patrick and Sylvia ignore him.

Eleven-sevenths of a block from their meeting place, Patrick looked up at the sky. He saw five eye-colored clouds heading left, and that the wind had become visible. Next, six cubic blocks' worth of buildings all disappeared. It was amazing. He felt dizzy and fell down again. As he tried to get up, two thirteen-car el trains roared by underneath him. Then everything went back to normal.

It began to rain viciously. Patrick cursed now,

twice, and ran under a building, then cursed once again. It was only his third date with Sylvia.

About thirty-five seconds went by, and Patrick got more and more nervous.

Sopping and beautiful, Sylvia snuck up behind him, already exerting pressure for Patrick to kiss her—just as he'd known that she would.

Patrick cursed for a fourth time, under his breath, then said hello. Sylvia's coat was flapping and snapping around her, and he had to admit she looked gorgeous. Closing her eyes, she presented her lips to him *right there in front of the building.*

Patrick kept his own eyes open and kissed her, watching two filthy posters blow by, then closed them, counting his curses. It was awful.

Then everything went back to normal.

The Shack Dwellers

An *asalto* was in progress on a hill around the corner from a row of shacks somewhere in south-central Mexico. Two Mexicans were taunting a gringo, purposefully shoving him around, and laughing. "Ha ha ha." The gringo lay in the dirt, cut, and with a case of bad diarrhea; he'd run out of doxycycline two days ago. He still had his money, but his vacation was ruined.

Mr. Vesuvius, a rich Costa Rican, interrupted advertently. "Boys, come now," he said. "Iron this out as guests in my sumptuous shack compound why don't you."

To this the gringo was very amenable, but the two muscular shack dwellers were not. Misconstruing (on purpose) the idiom, they did to Mr. Vesuvius what was almost bad Spanish for "iron out," then laughed. "Ha, ha ha ha. Ha ha."

To avenge himself, Mr. Vesuvius unsheathed his *machetazo* and with eight quick chops neatly severed the head of one of the Mexicans. Mr. Vesuvius and his bodyguards then bolted into the foliage. The remaining Mexican was stunned, mostly by the sight of his best partner's head wobbling around next to his shoe.

The gringo saw his chance now and took it. He, too, bolted, losing himself on purpose in the row upon row of shacks and crud, not stopping even briefly to play kick-the-head with the Mexican's head, as Mr. Vesuvius had.

The Mexican who still had his head buried (temporarily) both parts of his partner, then returned empty-handed to his shack to face his small starving family.

His young wife was nursing a starving infant; her breasts were opulent and full—unlike her small *jacalucho*—but their milk just was not all that nourishing. The Mexican gazed down at the two of them.

He and Jesus, he told her, crossing himself quickly, had failed to relieve a cruddy mick gringo of his dollars then kill him so that he could not go to the police on them then, blah blah blah. Interference also was called on Mr. Vesuvius.

The beautiful wife, on purpose, said nothing. It was too hot for talk in their shack now.

When siesta time passed, the Mexican took off his shirt, propped up his toes on a stool, and began a set of seventy-five diagonal *flexiones*, laughing in time to the strain. "Ha *ha*, ha *ha*, ha *ha* . . ." He was still in a mild state of shock.

From the cuffs of the Mexican's trousers, six bronze coins made the short drop to the soft dirt floor of the shack.

His young wife looked purposefully on as the brisk, useful exercises continued.

Ithaca

Aurora on in to Lake Michigan, from Floss-moor to Glencoe, King Panic reigns in fast forward. Be-lieve it. The Hawk has skipped town it's so hectic. While above the Sears Tower, on this foreshortened Tuesday of bright zero Indian summer, a chevron of mallards flies by, headed north by northwest toward the Arctic. On the streets it is no picnic either. Traffic's impacted on 294 and the Kennedy, not to mention the Ryan, the Edens, the Stevenson, Lake Shore Drive, and the Daley. People lie low along Cottage Grove, across 35th Street, up Halsted, but elsewhere it's one big stampede. The Magnificent Mile's a bad joke. Suicides bounce down the sides of the Hancock, finding the future in huge frantic gulps, while a single handheld Panasonic is catching the antics of gawk-ers. Looters and gropers are having a field day as well, getting trampled and crushed in the process, but still. And the Loop's a continuous frenzy. There's gunfire, bloodshed galore, and loud music, and countless premor-tem tableaux. For while in most other million-plus polises north of the Tropic of Cancer it's all but all over, in Chicago it's still just beginning.

Raymond Zajac, the principal lefthanded starter of the American League Champion Chicago White Sox, is standing in front of the thick oaken door of a three-story graystone at 1367 N. State Street. He knocks. Having emerged forty-six minutes ago from a Series IV coma, he has since been the victim of Type C amnesia. Painful braincramps, like a series of miniature aneurisms, have left him in a genuine fugue state, a man out of time. His entire past seems a dream of attractive young female physicians, NMR scans, violin scherzos, and blood tests, his future little more than the sickening hush you can always make out just before the bleachers collapse, or when someone won't answer the door. And, except for the upside down inside out orange T-shirt he's wearing, right leg down through the neckhole, left leg out through one sleeve, he is naked.

When nobody answers he knocks three more times, starts making a noise like a siren, knocks harder. He still doesn't have all the dots on his dice, and his chemoreceptor trigger zones desperately need to be stimulated. Braincell by braincell, in very slow motion, he's dying.

With his ear to the door now he listens for noises or voices inside, but there's nothing.

He curses.

Teresa Zajac goes into their upstairs and quickly begins to undress: she apparently can't hear the knocking. She has not had a shower or even a chance to change clothes since before Sunday's game, which is already—what? Almost forty-eight hours ago. She knows that it's anal-compulsive to be wanting to bathe at this juncture, but still. She's convinced she could deal with all this more effectively if she just felt less tranced-out and grungy.

Her body, at thirty-three years and nine months, is still lithe and taut, a teenager's really, but better, and there isn't a blemish or tan line corrupting her flushed Welsh-Slovakian skin. Her three-inch cropped hair is somewhere between red and brown: its exact hue depends on the light and how long it has gone sans shampoo. The only things wrong with her otherwise are her gnarled swollen knuckles, the rough patch of callous below her left jawline, and the pale blue half moon under each green-gray eye. She has not really slept for three days.

She gets into the shower, turns on the faucet, then gasps and jigs back as the pipes clang belch and rumble vituperatively before retching forth bursts of brown water. Then nothing.

She gets out of the shower and turns on the tap in the sink. The chromium nozzle burps a few times, coughs, but that's all.

Theresa just stands there. The door of the medicine cabinet hangs open to such a degree that she can't see her face in the mirror. What she sees is the shower stall's sliding translucent glass door and, in particular, the reversed silhouette of a knife-wielding wigged Norman Bates that Raymond had had stenciled on. As a joke.

She dries off her ankles and feet, puts her green Cornell sweatshirt back on, then pulls on clean cotton socks, blue and white panties, and blue jeans.

What she wants is for things just to go back to normal.

To normal.

Zajac's still cooling his heels on the doorstep. Still moaning, still fuguing, still dying. And the schizoid voices or voice in his head won't let up.

Forty-three hours ago, during the bottom of the third inning of the third game of the World Series, while making his first official appearance at the plate since coming into the major leagues fifteen years ago, Zajac was nailed above the right temple by a high inside cross-seamed fastball delivered by Reds lefthander Mason Marietta, this in retaliation for similar pitches by Zajac in the tops of the second and third, pitches which themselves had been prompted by Marietta's clearly intentional decking of Minth Lorenz, the Sox' MVP shortstop and leadoff man. In other words, for simply protecting his hitters. Then, as Zajac was being carted off the field on a stretcher, the game was further delayed by a thunderstorm. (A voice from the grandstand had deadpanned, "It's fixed!") Two hours and fifty-six minutes later it was officially postponed altogether. That was that. For as far as anyone can tell it was right around then, with the World Series deadlocked at one game apiece and the postponed game's score tied at zero, that World War III had been kindled, though the big international picture, of course, had not looked auspicious all summer. Things then got hectic. The upshot so far is that early this morning, as Zajac lay comatose in the intensive care unit of Wesley Memorial Hospital, a significant number of the principal cities north of the Tropic of Cancer were vaporized, wasted, obliterated. The rest was just endgame. By the time that he finally came to forty-nine minutes ago, Chicago was one of only four unhit cities of America's nineteen most populous, and all twelve MIRVed warheads on three Soviet INCRBIMs had already been launched toward the Loop. Disregarding biases generated by the various electromagnetic tornadoes, their approximate interval of launch to arrival was under one hour, the fact that had generated the Greater Chicagoland Area's transports of fast-forward chaos.

As far as Zajac could tell, however, the place where he finally came to was deserted, though he formed no opinion as to whether or not that was strange. He'd just raised his level of consciousness from Series IV comatose on up through stuporous, combative, agitated, and lethargic to alert but with Type C amnesia, all this in less than ten minutes. He sat himself up. It was dark. He was scared. He'd made it about two-thirds of the way out of bed before discovering that, by a number of means, he and the bed were connected. Woozy and fuguing like crazy, he nonetheless managed to untape and pull out the angiocath in his wrist, unfasten the trio of electrodes attached to his waist and his chest, then gingerly tug, coax, and yank the long Foley catheter out through his bladder, urethra, and penis. (There was still enough painkiller coursing through him to make this, though just barely, bearable.) Thus disconnected, he staggered and lurched down the hallway, using the walls for support, then descended the first set of stairs that he came to and emerged two flights down into panic.

Stripped somehow of his blue cotton gown in the frantic stampede to get into and out of the hospital, he was forced to fashion a pair of lopsided bloomers from the damp orange T-shirt (the Official Commemorative T-Shirt, in fact, of the umpteenth anniversary of Chicago's Great Fire) that he was lucky enough to discover in a trashcan outside. Oblivious to the incoming missiles, rattled and baffled by the continuous frenzy he found in the streets, he nonetheless managed to figure out where he (probably) lived by getting himself to a phonebook and looking up the address of the name he had found on his white plastic-coated ID bracelet, thanking Christ when he did that only one R J Zajac was listed. He'd've called the place first to see who might answer, but after two or three minutes of waiting he could not get a dial tone. The only and best thing to do, he now knew, was to go there. He also had enough on the ball to realize he should not trust his memory, so he tore out his page from the phonebook, folded it neatly, and tucked it down inside his bloomers.

Having a name and address made him feel somewhat better, but he still must've looked real beleaguered. For at this point, as if by some miracle, a gray-eyed blond-banged and -braided Guardian Angel in a scarlet beret appeared out of nowhere to help him. She listened to his address, gave him quick clear straightforward directions, patted his butt "for good luck," then faded back into the mob just as suddenly. And Zajac, dazed but unfazed, headed north by northwest toward the Hancock.

Walking or jogging the first couple of blocks and pedalling the rest of the way on a borrowed Schwinn ten-speed, he negotiated the mile and three-eighths from Wesley to Schiller and State as quickly as possible, following the Angel's expert directions and avoiding as well as he could a redundant but tempting succession of mondo bizarro end-of-the-world-as-we-know-it scenarios, and so ended up about a half hour later on the doorstep he hopes against hope is his own.

It has yet to dawn on him what's causing all the commotion, but in the state that he's in he really doesn't care that much either. He does have this tugging premonition that something untoward might go down, but to whom, why, or when he can't say. For now all he knows is that, having come all this way, he desperately wants to be home.

He starts to knock, stops, and starts groaning. Re-checks his ID bracelet, examines the page from the phonebook, stares at the door's pewter numerals. It all matches up. He fingers the puncture he left in his wrist when he pulled out his angiocath: it's turned black and blue and still hurts. His fist throbs from knocking, his tender urethra still burns. And inside his head now he swears he can feel something dripping.

* * *

Upstairs in their bedroom, Teresa is once again trying the nurses' station of Wesley's intensive care unit: 649-2737. She's already got the pathetic little seven-note melody memorized she's dialed it so many damn times, but so far all she's been able to get is a busy signal or, when it does ring, no answer. She's desperate to know how Ray's doing.

Both she and Jesse, their thirteen-year-old only son, had left Zajac's bedside less than eight hours earlier. The thirty-six hours before that had been one sleepless nightmare fantasia. Teresa had talked with reporters and doctors and teammates and nurses, kept vaguely apprised of the rumors, but had spent most of that time in with Ray, watching his lips or his eyes or the monitors for some sign of—what? She may as well have been kneeling down praying in the pew of some church for all the damn good it had done him. The nurses and doctors were eventually able to convince her that, while she was certainly welcome to stay, the best thing to do at that point (it was already two in the morning of her second night there) was to take Jesse home, get some sleep, then send Jesse to school in the morning and come back down by herself. In the meantime they promised to call her if there were even the slightest of changes and gave her the direct number into the nurses station in case she might have any questions.

It finally dawns on her now that the phone line is dead: no ringing, no recorded message, no dial tone. The white shaft of silence is splitting the back of her forehead. She hangs up, rechecks the number while waiting in vain for a dial tone, then starts dialing anyway. Dead. She bangs the receiver back into its cradle and curses. What's even harder to take is her quickening realization that, because of everything else that's transpired, there's simply no way any more she could get back down to Wesley in person.

She exhales, dries off her palms on her sweatshirt, starts gnawing the tip of her ring finger.

She can't believe all this is happening.

Alone in the kitchen, Jesse plows through the junk drawer for matches. There are none. What he pulls out instead is the yellowing Mother's Day card he'd made in third grade for Teresa. He unfolds it and reads it:

MOTHER

M mondo   musician   magnificent
O out of this world   outragess   outstanding
T thoughtfull   tremendess   terrific
H helpfull   happy   harmless
E excellent   enchanting   entertaining
R respectfull   relistic   remarkable

Love,
Jesse

He folds it back up and stuffs it down into his pocket, then continues to riffle the trilevel chaos for matches.

Teresa stands poised and erect in the fifteen-by-twenty-foot family room. Having just moved a step or so sideways, she's convinced she's now dead in the center. She's waiting. The 63-inch Sushiza TV screen buzzes and crackles with static while a canned-sounding voice continues to calmly announce that *This is a test. This station is con-*

*ducting a test of the Emergency Broadcasting System.
This is only a test.* She picks up the remote control thing
off the Einstein Moomjy Aberdeen Heather carpet and
starts changing channels. Each station's audio portion
consists of either a high-pitched test pattern or the only-a-
test admonition. Each station's picture shows nothing but
bright light and static. Exhausted but mesmerized, she
stands there and watches and listens.

Behind where she stands, on the wall over the
black Pantex couch, hangs Ed Paschke's *Gash,* an air-
brushed affair, mostly in cyans and yellows, of a pubes-
cent punk doing her darnedest to come off as bored to the
max but still trés intense: no easy trick when your face is
the color of a ripe avocado. To the left of the Paschke is
Braque's *Pitcher with newspaper, violin, and matchbox
(L'Indépendant),* a recently discovered 1912 oval collage.
Facing the Paschke on the opposite wall is *Sam's gun on a
green table,* Clar Monaco's rendition in fast goopy oils of a
radically cockeyed mongrel staring down hard at a six-
shooter, apparently trying to figure out what to do with it.
To the right of the Monaco is a mostly white untitled
abstract by Leona Insurance combining ornery slashes of
what looks to be car primer, wide bands of gesso, and
blood. Beneath these two canvases are four twelve-foot-
long walnut shelves designed and installed by Fred
Nagelbach. The top two are both solid albums, 2012
altogether, in scrupulously alphabetical order. The third
shelf holds magazines, catalogs, worstsellers, verse. The
bottom shelf's crammed tightly with scores, video car-
tridges, digital discs, and cassettes, plus Jesse's collec-
tions of Krapp, Krantz, and King. In front of the window,
facing back into the room, is Teresa's dad's old Stein-
way E.

Teresa finally snaps to, glancing up out of habit
at the battery-check light on the First-Alert smoke detec-

tor. As soon as she spots it, however, the glowing red point, after six years' continuous service, suddenly winks out and dies.

She runs her hands back through her oily hair, pulls on it, musses it up with a vengeance. *Stand by*. Her arms drop down next to her sides, her eyes close, and her trembling palms open out as she zeroes in hard on the Gespensterwellen and gets set to listen. *Tonbandstimmen unbekannte Herkunft. Please stand by*. Then she turns her hands over, raises her elbows away from her waist, and just freezes.

Zajac at last spots the doorbell: it's right where it should be, of course, embedded in the jamb plain as day at a point right in line with his elbow. He mentally palms himself in the forehead as it starts to sink in just how zonked he must be not to've noticed it earlier, then imagines the jolt he'd've felt if he'd actually palmed himself there. He exhales and inhales, summons what presence of mind he has left, then pushes the buzzer three times.

Fifteen seconds go by. No one answers.

And but then there's a noise, then a voice, then the creak of a foot on a stair. Information.

He knocks five more times, *dot da da dah dah*, leaving the familiar tatoo unresolved. He's excited.

He hears a chain rattle and a big deadbolt lock get released. There are voices. He's pushing his hair off his forehead, wondering six things at once, and contracting his abdominal muscles when the door gets pulled open and he finds himself facing a boy and, just behind him, a woman. The boy's face is bony, with grayish blue eyes. Pretty tall. The woman he really can't see yet.

The boy steps aside, blurting out something

110

that Zajac can't catch. He focuses in on the woman, taking her face in. Her eyes.

"How on earth," she starts saying. It's clear she is shocked. "Come in. Just come in."

He balks for a couple of seconds, hitches up the waist of his bloomers, goes in.

The boy shuts the door. "What's with the T-shirt?" he says.

But Zajac can't answer. Behind the boy's shoulder there's a strange little shelf sticking out from the wall of the foyer on which a foot-high Dalmation is sitting with one front paw raised and extended. It seems to be staring right at him—and begging. What he finds even stranger is that both shelf and Dalmation are painted with the same spotted black-on-white pattern.

"Hey," says the woman, to Zajac. She touches his famous cleft chin. "You okay?"

He blinks, smiles, and nods, trying to think what to say.

She puts her hands onto his waist and starts to embrace him, but he doesn't know how to react. It's her face. He thinks it's pure gorgeous, the best face he's ever laid eyes on, and he wants to believe it's his wife's. And to hold her. To have her. But his uncertain jitters and stiffness abort her attempt at the hug. He can't help it.

"Mondo?" she says.

They just stare at each other.

Then, without pressure or moisture, they kiss.

"I was in the hospital," he says, pulling back, trying to explain what has happened. "But so, I came home."

"You . . . came home," says the woman.

"How'd you get here," the boy wants to know. Shakes his head. "I mean, jeez."

Zajac can't say. All this excitement has brought back the pain in his head with a vengeance. He winces. He feels his heart blipping and seizing. He's white.

"So you know me," he says. He can just get it out.

The boy and the woman just look at each other, and but all of a sudden, to Zajac, they appear sort of greenish and much much much farther away. Out of focus.

"We *know* you?"

He starts to pass out. His mouth works to warn them, to ask for some help, but not much but moaning comes out. As his body torques sideways he tries to sit down, to break his collapse with his palms.

Doesn't work.

They lug him and drag him and carry him into the family room, where it's carpeted, then lie him down facing straight up. He's breathing but no longer moaning. They're scared.

Drip drip drip.

It occurs to Teresa that the head of his bed down at Wesley had been raised about thirty degrees, so she props up his neck with a pillow. But now what? About every half hour or so a nurse had come in and done things like pull back his eyelids to measure his pupils' dilation, or taken his pulse or his blood pressure, or tweaked one or both of his nipples. Teresa tries tweaking the left one, but since she really doesn't know what to look for, she stops and starts stroking his chest. Then his forehead. She's sweating. One nurse had checked for something she called the Babinski reflex by taking a stiff piece of cardboard and scraping the soles of his feet: if the toes on his left foot flared out, it meant there was irritation on the right side of his brain, and vice versa. Or something like that. She wishes she'd paid more attention to what the nurses and doctors were saying and doing instead of just sitting there watching Ray's face, or staring at the graph lines and blips on the monitors, or praying for him to come to. Because now that he has and come home, she doesn't have any idea what to do.

And Ray is now shaking all over. Drool's foaming up from between his clenched teeth, his eyes are rolled back in his head, there's blood oozing out his right ear.

Jesse can't take it. "Make it stop!" he insists. "Close his eyes!"

"Okay, okay. There." And she does it. It gives her the willies. She's crying. "Calm down!"

"Jesus," says Jesse. He stands up and shivers. He's white. It looks like he might start to vomit.

He does.

Teresa remembers that on the day she'd met Ray her elbows and knuckles were killing her. Even back then. It was a Tuesday, May 9, about 10:45 in the morning. His father was tuning Namgae's (her roommate's) piano and Ray'd come along for the company. For the first half an hour or so she hadn't even known he was there. She'd stayed down the hall in her bedroom, rehearsing her end of the allegrissimo movement of Prokofiev's *Back in the USSR* sonata, then had literally bumped into him as they were both on their way to the kitchen.

Ray was wearing a navy blue suit, a dark green silk tie, a pinpoint cotton blue shirt. (He'd just been on television.) He was tall. It looked like he'd just got a haircut.

In the kitchen he told her his name, what he

was doing there, asked if he might use the phone. His voice sounded nervous. His eyes were slate blue. She said yes.

She remembers all this very clearly, too clearly, as Ray now lays dying.

She remembers what she had on too: no socks or shoes, cut-off white Levi's, and a navy blue NYU sweatshirt. She had not washed her hair yet that morning, and for this she was silently cursing herself.

She never heard of Ray Zajac, but while her tea water boiled she eavesdropped right in on his call. The person on the other end of the line, some guy named Roberto, was the one doing most of the talking, so there wasn't a lot to find out. She remembers how much it relieved her that the person he'd called wasn't female.

Namgae then came into the kitchen and you could tell that she'd put on mascara. Ray said so long to Roberto and hung up the phone. He thanked Namgae, thanked Teresa, for letting him use it, then headed back out to the livingroom.

The kettle now started to whistle.

"Hey, want some tea?" called Teresa.

"Pluck me whilst I blush," Namgae whispered. In the three years Teresa had known her, it was the first time Namgae had spoken or behaved in a way even remotely suggestive of lust. And besides. She already had Dr. Hudson.

"Not really," said Ray. "Hey. But thanks," then headed again down the hallway.

Hey. But thanks.

Namgae and Teresa just looked at each other.

"O boy."

Fourteen months later their Jesso's been born. She remembers. How big he had felt but how small he had turned out to be.

She remembers that on the day she met Ray her old Lamee bow had just been rehaired with good Russian. She remembers having carefully wiped the used rosin from the strings and the fingerboard of the fiddle her father had bought her with the money from some weird insurance policy after her mother had died. Her Vuillaume.

She also remembers her absolute certainty that Namgae's tuner's tall son would soon call, that in spite of her absolute pitch and long years of practice and study her arthritis would end her career before it could really begin, and that these things would happen to *her*. She can actually picture herself

blip blip blip

Meantime, slumped in a whirlpool that same afternoon in the Comiskey Park visitors training room, the Ray she remembers was thoughtfully peeling and sectioning a thick-skinned pink grapefruit, a gift from some fan. He could picture Namgae. The Blue Jays were playing the White Sox that evening on local TV, but Ray was not pitching. He could picture Teresa. He put down the grapefruit, picked up his hard little black rubber ball, and started methodically squeezing. He did not like grapefruit. He wanted to pitch, and Teresa. On the other hand, Namgae wasn't all that bad either.

But the thing that concerned him the most was his season: his stats, his career, his whole future. Two weeks before, while making only his third start of the season, he'd badly torn a groin muscle while fielding a bunt on the slick artificial turf in Seattle and landed himself on the 21-day disabled list. Five or six starts down the tubes, just like that. It was his first real injury since his football days back in high school, and he wasn't real pleased. He'd continued traveling with the team, however: suiting up, playing pepper, charting pitches and scouting the other teams' hitters, trying to make himself useful for the incredible salary the Blue Jays were already paying him. And his teammates were winning: 9-4 since he'd left the rotation, 13-6 overall, with ten of those wins on the road. What killed him was not knowing what might not happen, or happen, to *him*.

It was only his second full season. He'd been 18-8 as a rookie, with a 2.64 ERA, a 7.85 MBA, and 239 strikeouts. The sabermetricians went crazy. He'd also pitched four one-hitters, a record, of which he'd only won two, which was also a record. American League Rookie of the Year by a landslide. Two *Sports Illustrated* covers: one solo, the second with three other Blue Jays. Missed the Cy Young Award by six votes.

What he wanted most desperately now was to keep all this up, to recover and still have his stuff. There was no real good reason, of course, to assume that he wouldn't, but still. He tried not to think about that, to wonder instead about calling Namgae or Teresa. He'd taken their number from his father's little green clients address book, but he didn't know which one would answer.

He got out of the whirlpool, covered himself with a towel, and was snapped by two more as he walked to his locker. He yanked off his own and snapped back. A red plastic floor-hockey puck hit his shin and ricocheted into his locker. He retrieved it and fired it back at the shooter. A *Sun-Times* reporter wanted to know how his groin was. He turned round and belched. Then he sat down and plunged his left fist, wrist, and forearm into his portable barrel of rice, clenching and twisting and driving with all of his frustrated might. He was thinking.

He'd already been given two nicknames: The Canada Arm (which he lost four years later when his agent finally got him into a pitcher's park and he signed with the

White Sox for what came to just under his weight in pure gold the first year, then went up) and Gamma Ray Zajac. The second one stuck. The ray in question referred to his high riding hummer that brought the white ball from the cross-seamed release point of his hard-to-read three-quarter lefthanded buggywhip delivery to the heart of the heart of the strike zone—although sometimes above and inside it—at (according to Ted Turner's SzorcGun at least) 98.59 miles an hour. In about a third of a second, in other words, about the time it took hitters to blink.

Or to duck. Because that was the thing about Ray, even then. In addition to having decent control of his foshball and screwgie, he was also real wicked and sudden. Or, as Don Drysdale had rhetorically wondered that Tuesday on Channel 32 while reviewing the Blue Jays' rotation: "Does young Mr. Zajac have a control problem or's he just flat *mean?*" Drysdale then chuckled and snorted as the station had segued to Warner Wolf's comic slow-motion montage of Zajac upending a half dozen batters. For the fact of the matter was that in 234.2 innings the previous season Ray had walked only forty-nine batters, twenty intentionally, but had *hit* thirty-six. "Ray'll come at you," his manager, Roberto Raritan, had admitted the previous evening to Howard Cosell on Monday Night Baseball. "There's no doubt about it. But tactical jamming systems are strictly preëmptive, ad hoc, and since velocity and location are the matrix mechanics of pitching, there's always that trace of uncertainty." Cosell'd said, "Say what?" and then cackled. Ray's own rationale for the media—when they forced him to give one—was that, while he never had thrown at a hitter on purpose, if he saw a guy really dig in he would naturally start to get nervous and was thus prone to lose some control. Jays catcher Vin Da Capo had put it less coyly for a *Sporting News* feature on Ray: "Sucker comes up tries to sit on Ray's smoke we fug him and play him some chin music." Drysdale, himself a notorious headhunter back in his playing days with the Dodgers, had summed it up thusly to an amused Kenny Harrelson as the montage of knockdowns concluded: "Listen, it's always been part of the game, Hawk. You know that." Harrelson whewed and agreed. "Yessir," he drawled. "That ol fear of music. Though you *know* the kid pulled this kind of stuff over in the National League, where he'd have to stand in and hit for himself, he'd last about what? Three or four innings at most."

Teresa, of course, was watching this broadcast with interest, even though she'd never been much of a sports fan till Namgae'd tipped her off about Ray after he and his father had left. There she was, nonetheless, crouched on the edge of the sofa, munching unsalted cashews, alone—Namgae had just lost a coin flip and been forced to dash the half block to Gim Bop's and pick up their orders of be bim bop—doing her darnedest to make what these two hick announcers were saying make sense, when lo and behold the young Mr. Zajac himself called her up, just as she'd known that he would. (The Gespensterwellen she always stayed keyed to had never been stronger or clearer.) Ray had been able to sneak from the dugout in the top of the second and was using the payphone outside the visitors' locker room. It was eight after eight, almost exactly nine hours since they'd seen one another, and Teresa's nervous and calm systems were suddenly both in an uproar. As were, of course, Ray's, only worse. But Teresa remembers that before he could even get started with his hemming and hawing she came straight out and asked him what chin music was. And, hawing and hemming, he told her.

    blip blip

    Teresa and Ray are on much the same

wavelength apparently, because this same conversation has begun to come back to Ray too, but with one big big difference: while Teresa can picture their whole long first Tuesday together in detail, all Ray can recall through the damp gauzy veil of his fugue state are the distinctly un-visual contours of some nervewracking phonecall, then nothing, as the stuporous neurons in his pineal gland and his pons mince ritardando on laser-sharp edges of coma. *Drip drip.* A slightly less floppy mnemonics, however, would go on to reveal that the nervewracking phonecall led directly to dinner that very same night up at Grunts, as we segue again (flashing back day for night through undulating midnight blue filter) to:

Their virtually simultaneous arrival in two separate taxis at the corner of Park West and Dickens. Ray had on a tight black knit Izod shirt and almost new Levi's. No belt. His definition and muscle tone were simply astonishing, but he still didn't look unintelligent. Teresa was fetching in Namgae's clingy black Gore-Tex skirt, very short, and a plain white men's cotton T-shirt. Perfume by Issey Miyake. Their hair was still wet. With put-on sangfroid they proclaimed they were starving, went in. Two people recognized Ray, but he suavely declined to sign autographs.

They were given a booth in the corner. Ray ordered sole, Teresa the mushroom bleu-cheeseburger. The busboy poured water. Teresa looked under the ashtray and discovered a CTA transfer. She folded it, played with it, saved it (still has it, in fact, in some drawer). They smiled at each other. Preliminary dialogue continued to be awkward and tentative (they mocked the decor, for example, proclaimed once again they were starving), but as they were standing in line for the salad bar they somehow got onto Ray's father, the half-blind old tuner who'd got them together. And that broke the ice.

119

Teresa was touched by the fact that when the Blue Jays played games in Chicago Ray always stayed in the condo he'd bought for his Dad on Pine Grove: smack in the center of Buttland, she noted. Ray's Dad was fifty, Teresa's just seven months younger. Both of their mothers were dead, it turned out: both of cancer. Neither had brothers or sisters but always had wanted them, and both had been born in the fifties. They relaxed. Subsequent conversation touched on Anderson, Carter, the Blue Jays, the service, the salad, the President's three cardiologists, Namgae Kim, Dr. Hudson, inexpensive imitation 1952 Fender Telecasters, beta shades, urban sax, bottom, Richard Nixon, stiff plastic discs, and the blues, but eventually and inevitably on "putting a little hair on the ball" and "showing a guy Bobby Brown," which Ray "sort of" supposed were the "principal canon" of his "private religion." Teresa was charmed but dismayed. She found this "too strange." Ray tried to drop it, but she just wouldn't let him. (She was really impressed by this big hunk's vocabulary in discussing such violent behaviour.) She ironically begged to hear more about "clunking guys" upside the head "for no earthly reason at all." By now Ray was much too embarrassed. He started to detail instead the subtle advantages of being left-handed in baseball and racquet sports, but Teresa would not be put off. She mentioned the cello—confounding him further—then told him pointblank he was "cruel"— she'd meant to say "mean"—quoting Drysdale. "And what's this about fear of music?" What could Ray say? Eye contact and body language were held to a minimum for the next several minutes. Ray tried to wax euphemistic: the result was a series of silences each more discrete than the last one. They tried to talk music again, but Ray's jockish tastes were revealed to be too unsophisticated. Neither Teresa's barely clothed singularities or Ray's bulging and naked left forearm ever came up. Nor did the latter's groiner or the former's arthritis. It was tense. The ice was once again broken, however, when the latest bad Jesus joke was expertly sprung by Teresa (apropos of Ray's frank admission that "Jeez, am I nervous," she bigly admitted that she too was nervous then gnawed on the back of her palm and asked him, "Who's this?" Ray was too rattled to guess. Teresa kept gnawing: "I mean, speaking of *nervous*, who's this?" But Ray had no clue. "Jesus biting his nails," said Teresa) and which Ray, at first, didn't get, but then found so awful he gagged on his sole, snorting out some through his nose. The food was okay. The service was fine. Neither one smoked after dinner because neither of them was on fire. (That one was Ray's.) Lime-flavored bombes topped with chocolate were ordered by both for dessert but just picked at. Check paid by Ray, tip by Teresa. No drinks.

Back at Teresa's apartment (which Namgae had graciously vacated) they listened sedately to Priaulx Rainier's "Quanta" and, less sedately, to Nile Mansions' cover of "Talk Talk," but somehow wound up tilted elbow to elbow over Namgae's old Baldwin for what was apparently, for Teresa at least, some dead serious, unsedate arm wrestling. Ray was victorious in four out of seven (righthanded) and Teresa was thereby compelled, according to groundrules laid down beforehand, to drop down posthaste on the carpet and give him six bona fide flexiones, exposing to Ray in the process a scratch on her thigh and the backs of her scrumpdiddleyumptious pink knees. Two awkward moments now followed, but Ray in the end got his chance to examine all the little doodads and things in Teresa's strange bathroom. It was Teresa's turn next, and she gargled. Later, strained groin and all, Ray was shamed, barely, by a gadulka-wielding Teresa into a macho jock's version of a truncated Slovakian czardas, leaving Teresa with no choice at all but to notice his sturdily independent rear-end suspension system and how it just might allow for some extraordinary performance and handling. In a word, their respective excitements were mounting.

They kissed for the very first time at 2:22. They were still in the livingroom, dancing to no song at all, jammed up against one another. By 2:26 they were more or less prone on Teresa's made bed. It was here that the certain lengths to which neither were prepared to go in order to facilitate innovative sexual intercourse between consenting adults remained unascertained, thus giving lie to the rumors that classical musicians of the female persuasion were frigid and that Polish men made terrible lovers because they insisted on waiting until the swelling went down. Love then took over and launched them on slippery particles of ecstasy into waves of celestial light, and they realized that nothing mattered at all except that as woman and man they were one, for now and throughout all eternity.

Yeah.

What Jesse remembers is similar but light years more recent, from this very same morning in fact, not to mention about ten times more awesome and sexy. What'd happened is this. On the way out of school, after weeks of procrastinating, he'd finally got up enough nerve to walk home with Maggie Mullova, the new girl at school, even though he'd sworn to himself about a googolplex number of times not ever to try such a thing. This was different.

The teachers had let them out early and Jesse knew why. (So did Maggie.) Even still, they'd moseyed the block and a half from the Latin School to Maggie's stepfather's apartment without once ever mentioning "it." The fact of the matter was that there really wasn't a whole lot of anything that Jesse could think of to say to her.

Some whited-out public school kid had lurched by on North with Hendrix's version of "The Star-Spangled Banner" feeding back hard on itself, wha-wha-whanging and bursting and toggling from a battered old Sanyo MX. (It was the first and last time either Jesse or Maggie would hear it.) Then silence. Dumb silence. It killed him.

"So where you going?" he said, even though he already knew.

"Home I guess. Nowhere," said Maggie. "Where *you* going?"

"Home?"

"Yeah I guess so."

"You're going home then, you mean?"

"I guess so. I mean, aren't you?"

Then it happened. They stopped on the sidewalk just around the corner from Maggie's stepfather's apartment, fiddled with each other's fingers, and kissed. Killerdiller. Their tongues even touched but as soon as they did something strange happened, a quickening flavor that drew them against one another, made them tilt sideways and back.

That was awesome, thought Jesse, still holding on to her fingers. I mean, that was really incredible.

"I gotta go in now," said Maggie, grinning a little. "Like I really do have to go in now."

Teresa is doing her darnedest not to break down. Not to talk to herself. To talk to herself, but just not out loud. To figure out what she should do.

She stands into spiraling vertigo. Her son's run upstairs, but she doesn't remember what for. To get help? That's a laugh. Did he say? To be able to die on his own?

She does not have the will now to wonder. Her unconscious husband's laid out on the carpet, a ludicrous orange-clad sculpture thrown into high relief by available light and her headache, his familiar proportions now angled obliquely below her, skewed by her weird point of view. She can't stand to look any more.

When something is bothering her, under normal conditions at least, there are measures she brings into play more or less automatically to help make her feel better. The first thing she does is imagine herself as vividly and concretely as possible at the moment that will signal once and for all the end of what's bothering her, the point at which the unpleasure of the present will be officially past. What this does is gives her an actual time-and-space episode to start looking forward to. Next she promises herself to remember having looked forward to it once it has finally occurred. To help guarantee she'll remember, however, she first must come up with a mnemonic nexus, an associative cue she can count on to jog her memory of the original promise at the point of the unpleasure's passage.

The way that she helps herself cope with her bouts of premenstrual syndrome is as good an example as any of how all this works. The four or five days before she gets her period are not her best time of the month. Her forehead breaks out, her left breast gets tender, and her thighs and her guts and her joints and her throat all feel so swollen and oinkly that sometimes she can't hardly stand it. It's sickening. What's worse is the accompanying churn in her brain that makes her feel eminently capable of furious barehanded manslaughter over even the most trivial incident: fans calling Ray, flies in the house, Jesse's dumb haircuts. In other words, nothing. The mnemonic nexus thus becomes the enormous relief she knows she will feel when the thick backed-up blood finally starts soaking down out through her uterus. The relief she will feel in the future she uses to neutralize, or pay back, or cancel—or something—the discomfort she feels in the present. In the meantime, of course, she still has the physical symptoms, but she's much better off psychologically if she's able to zero in hard on their absence. Because the harder she concentrates now, the better she's able to savor the counterpoint between how clogged-up and buggy she feels at the moment and the glorious mollification she knows she will feel when the blood comes.

Similarly, during Ray's West Coast road trips the nexus is meeting his plane at O'Hare. Or, when her arthritis starts to get out of hand, it's Dr. Czyzinski's white-on-white waiting room and the subsequent bliss of the cortisone.

The measures are based on her theory that it does you no good at all in the long run for unpleasure to merely have passed if its passing goes unnoticed and, as a result, uncelebrated. She does not have a name for these measures, but she tends to think of them as a practical attempt to make virtues of certain adversities: pure antecedent and consequent, only worked in reverse. They admittedly fail to make premenstrual syndrome or rheumatoid arthritis attacks any less irritating, they don't even make them go away any faster, but they do make them slightly less hard to put up with.

For the last thirty seconds Teresa's been doing her best to deploy these same measures in response to her current unpleasure. The problem, of course, is that the only way they might be effective is if she can somehow convince herself in good faith that there's even the remotest of chances that she, Ray, and Jesso will not have to die—that everyone won't have to, really—and that things just might go back to normal. And but so far she hasn't been able to.

"What I find most astonishing," she says, to herself. Then she stops, breathes in deeply, and exhales.

She holds out both palms, turns them over, then closes her eyes and just freezes for seventeen seconds.

One of Ray's face muscles twitches. That's all.

Eyes back wide open, still shaky, she squats on the floor by the bookshelves and thumbs through the racks of cassettes.

Let there be fiddles, she thinks.

Jesse announces he's booking.

"Just got to," he says, at the door.

"Where to?" says Teresa. "And why?"

"Maggie's," says Jesse. His breath reeks of vomit and Scope. "I just got to."

"Now listen," she says, though by this point there's really not much that can phase her. "Wouldn't it really be better—"

They hug.

"Just try to be careful out there."

"I'll be back."

She knows that he won't, but she nods, says okay.

She even begins to let go.

Ray's current level of consciousness is comatose. Impossible to arouse by verbal stimulation or kisses. Flexing and localizing movements (MOEX2): none at all. Response to tactile stimulation such as tweaking or twisting of nipples: none at all. Internal audio portion: what sounds like a zither with seven silk strings being plucked through a phaser, glissando. Positive Babinski response on right sole. Best verbal response: none at all. Pupils fixed and dilated to 8.5 millimeters. Luminosity of internal visuals:

126

pitch. Posterior tibial pulse: 110/20. Ventricular tachychardia tending toward cardiac standstill.

When Teresa inserts the cassette she's selected into Ray's new Nakamichi Dragon ZX (complete with six wolfram-trioxide heads, Z-zero phase error, DD Double Dolby, user-friendly zigzag control panel, and automatic azimuth correction) she discovers there's no more electricity. So what else is new, she can't help but wonder, as she lurches and hobbles upstairs to find Jesse's crummy (but battery-powered) old Vox Box.

What's on this cassette, unless she's mistaken, is a hybrid version of Beethoven's Fugue in B minor with the voice of the first violin left purposefully missing. Teresa had taped it back when she was still at the Conservatory off the copy of a friend of Namgae's who had gone to the Juilliard and whose professors had recorded it to provide their more advanced students with a challenging sequence of pitches to practice against. Or something like that: Teresa no longer remembers. A kind of makeshift bootleg play-along-with-the-Juilliard, then. Not the actual Robert Mann Juilliard, of course, with that dashing Joel Grossman on cello. But still.

She's excited.

Zajac comes to. It's a miracle. He even remembers his father, albeit briefly. The merest of glimmers of features, then nothing. He does not remember his son.

He looks at his wife, who is kneeling beside him, inserting a tape in a deck. In a hot flash of nausea, nostalgia, and pain he remembers the contours of a similar episode, but without too much verisimilitude. And then, again, nothing.

Opening riffs, minus the first violin, *Grosse Fuge*, volume dial turned down to three.

He rubs his right eye with the butt of his palm, hears the bloodshot conjunctiva toggle and creak with the fiddles, the dripping behind it continue. He's dying and knows it.

The exposition of the subject is driven ahead energetically, and he hears the three voices. He hears them and knows them. He senses that one voice is missing.

He notices floaters in his vitreous humor as he focuses in on his wife. He wonders if the static and hum in his head's from the tape. It is not.

The *Fuge* now hits fever pitch. Never mind.

He stares at Teresa's strange hair. At her eyes. At the line of her cheekbone. At the disarmingly wonderful gist of her breast through her shirt.

Nevermore.

The curtains are drawn, so it's dark in the family room now, more or less. And Jesse and Ray are both gone. Eyes open, scared, Teresa is listening hard to the tripled attack of the fiddles, getting set to stay dead a long time.

She turns up the Vox Box to nine, touches Ray's forehead, rests her bare neck on his shoulder. She can tell from the Gespensterwellen that it's going to come any second.

Okay. Her gnarled, knobby fingers stir at her sides, fretting and bowing saltando along with the dismembered fugue. Any time.

Jesus, she thinks. That nervewracking hush between notes we'd forgotten. Our sentence, I guess.

To wonder with all of our might. To remember.

We lie here and wait for the light.

About the Author

James McManus is the author of *Out of the Blue* and *Chin Music*, both novels. His work has appeared in *New Directions, TriQuarterly, Oink, Another Chicago Magazine* and elsewhere. He received a National Endowment for the Arts fellowship in poetry, 1980 and in prose, 1985. He received the Illinois Arts Council Fiction Award of 1982, 1983 and 1984. He teaches at The School of the Art Institute of Chicago.